Books by Richard Helms
Geary's Year
Geary's Gold
The Valentine Profile
The Amadeus Legacy
Joker Poker
Voodoo That You Do
Juicy Watusi
Wet Debt
Naked Came the Flamingo (contributor)
Paid In Spades
Bobby J.
Grass Sandal
Cordite Wine
The Daedalus Deception
The Unresolved Seventh
The Mojito Coast
Six Mile Creek
Thunder Moon
Older Than Goodbye
Brittle Karma

RICHARD HELMS

BRITTLE KARMA

an Eamon Gold novel

BLACK ARCH BOOKS

*A small portion of this novel originally appeared in Ellery Queen
Mystery Magazine (May-June, 2018) under the title "The King of
Gonna"*

For Elaine

Always for Elaine

ONE

There is a federal prison in Wyoming which you've probably never heard about, where thirty years ago inmates staged a doomed insurrection against the corrections officers.

The government response was fast, efficient and brutal. Eight of the inmates died—badly—in a ten-minute period. The rest spent the next six months in solitary confinement.

To prevent any further outbreaks, the prison superintendent declared a twenty-three hour a day lockdown. Inmates were allowed out of their cells for one hour each day, to shower or steal a few treasured moments in the sunshine. Communications between prisoners were kept to an absolute minimum, lest some small groups might attempt to plan another uprising.

The lockdown was never terminated. To this day, it remains in effect.

Abner Carlisle's skin was a translucent blue. It was the kind of skin you earn sitting in a six-by-eight concrete block cell for twenty-three hours a day over three decades. The years had rendered the melanin in his epidermis essentially inactive. A network of pulsating bluish veins crisscrossed his flesh like a rural road atlas. He reminded me of blind albino fish in ponds deep inside Kentucky caverns. His eyes were a milky blue. His hair was silvery-gray. He never smiled.

Abner Carlisle gave me the creeps.

"His name was Edward Rice," Carlisle said.

"Was?" I said.

"I can't find him anywhere."

"It's been thirty years," I said. "Perhaps he's dead."

"Thirteen million dollars can buy a lot of vanishing."

"Yes," I said.

"There were five of us. We worked on this plan for over a year, off and on. We knew the schedule for the armored car right down to the minute. Chucky Ells, he was the inside man. Eddie Rice was the wheel man. Me, Nat Pietke, and Jerzy Podnow were to pull off the actual robbery. It was supposed to take no more than six minutes, start to finish. How were we supposed to figure in something totally random like a cop car with a flat tire?"

"Best laid plans," I said.

"Killing the cop was the big mistake. That was Jerzy. Son of a bitch always goin' off half-cocked. He'd have sucked the green gas for it if cancer didn't get him first. Chucky Ells hung himself rather than go to prison. The rest of us went down on the federal charges. Eddie was the only one who never saw any time inside. He got away with the money, and I haven't seen him for over a quarter century."

"How'd he skate?"

"It was a mutual decision. Nate, Chucky and me decided that we'd keep his name out of it. By the time the cops caught up with us, Eddie had run off to stash the take. Thirteen million dollars. Where in hell would you hide something like that?"

I shrugged my shoulders.

"Someplace big," I suggested.

"He said he knew how to do it. He visited us from time to time in the joint. Then, about twenty-five years ago, he vanishes. Haven't seen him since. We got internet in prison about five years ago, and I learned how to use it. Tried to track him down through the web, but no luck. Two weeks I spent my one hour of free time looking for him on the computer. No showers, no sunlight. Damned near drove me crazy. Never found a trace of him. It's like he just disappeared. The last time I spoke with him, he was talking about leaving California with a woman, setting up in another state. He was always on the run, tired of looking over his shoulder. He promised me he would keep in touch, let me know where he was. Then, nothing."

I picked a pen up from my desk and drew random circles on the legal pad in front of me.

"You want me to find this Eddie Rice character?" I said.

"I'm the only one left. You know what it's like to die in prison, Mr. Gold?"

"No."

"It's the worst thing can happen. Guy dies inside the walls, and everyone knows it. It agitates the population. The bulls and the brass know it, too. They keep an eye on the really sick inmates. They let me see Jerzy the day he died. He looked awful. He was one huge tumor stitched together with a little skin and bone. It really had a hold on him. The superintendent was there too and told Jerzy he wouldn't die behind bars. Jerzy begged to let me go with him when they took him out, but that was against the rules. When the doctor told the superintendent it was time, they loaded Jerzy onto a gurney, wheeled him into an ambulance, and drove it just outside the walls. They parked facing the prison and opened the back so he could see the fields on the outside. That's where he died. For five minutes, he was free."

"What about the other guy? Nate?" I asked.

"He didn't last the first year. Got in a fight during recreation. Guy broke his neck for him. That was when they put in the extra fencing in the yard. Now inmates get recreation, but they don't get contact with the other prisoners. It's still a cage, but at least it's got fresh air."

"That leaves you and Eddie Rice."

"Can you find him, Mr. Gold?"

I tapped the pen against the legal pad as I framed an answer.

"Here's my advice," I said. "The next guy you tell this story to, maybe you should leave out some details."

"What?"

"I can read between the lines, Mr. Carlisle. I'm very good at what I do. If I take this case, I'll find Eddie Rice. When I do, you plan to park an ounce of lead between his eyes for abandoning you. Who do you think is going to take the heat as an accomplice? Sorry, sir, but I think I'll take a pass on this one."

"There's something I haven't told you."

"I'll bet there's a lot you haven't told me."

"The woman Rice ran off with is my daughter."

Maybe that should have changed things.

It didn't, of course, but maybe it should have.

"Tell you what," I said, as I wrote down a name and number. "There's this guy across town. He's very good. I really don't like him much, but I owe him one. I'll refer you to him."

I tore the slip from my pad and handed it to him.

He looked at it, his crepe paper skin drawn tight across his bony face.

He crumpled the paper, tossed it back on my desk, and walked out of my office.

I picked up the wad, dropped it in the round file, and turned my chair around to watch the pretty sailboats tack back and forth on the bay.

TWO

I had recently finished a plumbing job in Silicon Valley, plugging a leak at a cell phone company through which several hundred thousand dollars worth of chips had disappeared over six months. The owner of the company was very pleased with my work, since I'd also recovered most of the chips from a self-storage in San Bruno. He had written me a very generous check. I really didn't have to scare up much work for a couple of months.

I squired Heidi Fluhr to dinner at the Cliff House. Afterward, we took in a new Marc Chagall traveling show at the Museum of Modern Art. Heidi owns the art gallery downstairs from my office and is a first-nighter at all the local galleries and museums. I don't care much for modern stuff. My artistic temperament runs more toward Steve Ditko and Jack Kirby. I didn't tell Heidi this, of course. It wouldn't have mattered if I had. Heidi goes pretty much her own way, and a lot of the time I'm just along for the ride.

Heidi and I had been together for several years. We still hadn't decided what we were doing, exactly. Most of the time, we just revolved around each other in our separate orbits. I do what I do, she does what she does, frequently we do it together, and that about sums up the whole relationship. We have similar tastes in food, wine, and sex. Neither of us harbors much in the way of delusions of permanence. It makes for a comfortable arrangement. It's good for right now, and that's good enough for us.

On the night of the Chagall opening, Heidi was particularly fetching in basic black and not much of it. In heels, Heidi stands just shy of six well-packed feet. She shops the plus size racks, because she doesn't spend half her life kneeling in a stall with her finger down her throat. There's not a lot of fat on her frame, except where you want it to prove without a doubt she's a woman, and to keep the cuddling experience nice and cushiony. She's a big, healthy, blonde, Northern European goddess who turns heads wherever she goes, including the museum as she and I cruised from one painting to another.

We parked in front of a blue picture called *Creation*. It looked like finger-painting.

"The emotion is striking, but the real impact comes from its impulsivity," Heidi said, the faint German accent from her childhood making her voice rise and fall like a sleeping man's chest. "This is spontaneous, like Zen calligraphy. You can see the speed in the work. That comes from deliberating over it for some time, until it is concretized in his mind. The act is over in an instant, but the preparation might take months."

"Isn't that, more or less, the opposite of impulsivity and spontaneity?" I asked.

"Not in the art world. The act of creation is the instantaneous genius that follows contemplation and meditation."

"Uh-huh," I said. "Why does that strike me as the same kind of self-important blather that labels a wine *impetuous*?"

"Philistine," she said, and we moved on.

7

"Guy came by the office today," I said.

"The one with the milky skin?"

"Do you miss anything?"

"Not much. What did he want?"

"He's looking for a guy who helped him knock over an armored car thirty years ago."

"Does he want to kill this guy?"

"Why do you ask?"

"Because the guy is missing, and he has all the money."

"You *don't* miss much."

"I watch television. I know things. I suppose you didn't take the case."

I think she listened to me with just one ear, as she ran her eyes over Chagall's *Blue Donkey* the way a cop frisks a teenaged shoplifter.

"I didn't," I said.

"Good," she said, and we moved on.

THREE

You know how it goes. Every once in a while, you run up
on a guy who figures he just isn't dying fast enough.

Tuesday morning brought a call from Doogie Portnoy.
Doogie is a bail bondsman with an office near the Civic
Center. He's a well-heeled scuzzball, but he pays his bills on
time, and he doesn't make me eat with him.

"Got a skip for you." he said over the telephone.

I reached for my pen.

"Name?"

"Riley Quinch."

I put the pen down.

"Again?" I said.

"You think he'd learn. He got popped driving a stolen
Camry in SoMa. I wrote his bond, and he promised me he'd
show in court this time."

"So, revoke him."

"I'd like to find another way. The arraigning judge had a
hard-on for him. Riley's mother had to guarantee the bail
with her house. She's a nice lady. She used to give me
cookies when I was a kid in the neighborhood."

I thought it over. I was bucks-up. Chasing a life-long
miscreant like Riley Quinch sounded like a headache on top
of a toothache. Doogie was steady business, though. My cash

flow likes steady business. I wasn't the only P.I. in San Francisco. If I took a pass, Doogie might look elsewhere with the next skip.

"What was Riley's bail?"

"Judge laid on him hard, since he's habitual. Set the bond at twenty-five grand."

I'd get a tenth of that for hauling Riley in. On top of a nice check I'd just received for the cell phone job, I'd make my nut for the year.

"Okay," I said.

"There's a warrant out for Riley, too. Judge wants to hit him with contempt."

"Sounds reasonable. Not many people have more contempt for the court than Riley Quinch."

FOUR

My office is on the top floor of a two-story concrete office building off Richmond Street near Hyde Pier. I can see the Golden Gate Bridge and Mt. Tam from my window, when they aren't shrouded in fog. Right underneath me is Heidi's art gallery.

Heidi was just opening as I hit the street. She smiled when she saw me, probably remembering our marathon the night before. Romping with Heidi keeps me in shape for chasing bad guys all over the Bay area.

"Hello, lover," she said. "Wanna grab some breakfast? I can lock up again."

"Sorry. On the job. Doogie has a skip for me."

"Anyone I know?"

My door may read '*Eamon Gold, Discreet Investigations*', but Heidi and I have to talk about *something*. She's familiar with a lot of my regulars, if only by name and history.

"Riley Quinch ducked out on a court date again. When I run him down, it will mean a nice payday."

"Goodie. I love generous men who've come into money."

It took me half an hour to get to the Quinch residence in Noe Valley. At one time, the neighborhood had played host to hundreds of lower income families who lived in modest cottages and worked as hack drivers and custodians and kindergarten teachers. In the 1970s, you could buy in with an annual income of only ten grand or so.

No longer. Like almost every 'hood within the city limits, gentrification had come to Noe Valley. Even though it was only a three-bedroom, one-story house, putting the Quinch place up for a twenty-five-thousand-dollar bond was the equivalent of collateralizing a new car loan with the Hope Diamond. If Riley's mother sold the house, she could probably retire on the proceeds and live the rest of her life in comfort just about any place around the southern bay except the city.

Vonda Quinch was in her early sixties. She was plump but not obese. Standing a hair over five feet, she looked a little like a female version of Lou Costello. She wore a floral house dress and eyeglasses with pointed rims, suspended around her neck with a gold-plated chain. She fit into the increasingly upscale neighborhood that surrounded her the way an elephant would blend in at a cotillion. When she saw me, she sighed.

"Mr. Gold," she said.

We had a history. I'd dragged Riley in more times than I owned fingers.

"Sorry to disturb you," I said. "You know why I'm here."

"You'd better come in." She had a voice like a Munchkin.

She held the screen door open as I walked in and led me to the living room. It looked the same as it had the last time I'd been there—dingy, shopworn, and dusty. She started talking with her back to me, before we even sat down.

"I must be crazy," she said.

"Ma'am?"

"Putting my house up to get Riley out of jail. I should have known it would come to tears."

"It's not that desperate, yet," I said. "I'll find him. I always do. You'll lose your cash bond, but you'll keep the house."

Since Riley's bail had been twenty-five large, she'd had to pay a bit over thirty-seven hundred in cash to get him out. Her house covered the remainder.

"I'm not so certain this time," she said. "Riley is...different. He's been hanging around some very bad people. I don't like them, no I don't. Not a bit."

"What sort of people?" I asked.

"Well, you know Riley hasn't ever had a lot of friends. He was a sweet boy, but people took advantage of him. I suppose he decided one day that it wasn't worth getting close to people, so he distanced himself. I've only heard him mention three or four people he knows by name in the last several years. Suddenly, he's talking about all these young men he's going around with, and a mother knows, Mr. Gold. A mother knows."

"Knows what?"

"Why, that they're up to no good. He brought one of these boys around a couple of weeks ago. Rough looking fellow. He had rings and studs and all sorts of metal in his face and ears. And tattoos. In my day, only sailors had tattoos."

I didn't see the point in telling her tattoos were the height of fashion. Didn't want to turn her entire world view topsy-turvy.

"Do you recall this young man's name?"

"Of course. A mother keeps track of her children's friends. Gordy Carlton. That was his name."

"You know where he lives?"

"No. Why?"

"Riley isn't staying here. He needs a place to crash. He doesn't have a lot of friends, so he might be staying with this Carlton guy."

"I hope not. I don't like him. He looked dangerous. And he wore a shirt with a horrible picture on it."

"Picture?"

"It was a silhouette, but I could tell what it was. It was a man hanging from the mouth of a huge wolf. Just awful."

"Yeah. Awful," I said, and I meant it. I knew that picture. It was the logo for the Bottom Boys—which, when you think about it, was an unfortunate gang name in San Francisco. It came from The Bottom, a neighborhood between two hills in Hunter's Point. It was the kind of place you'd go to dump a fresh body. The Bottom Boys controlled most of the illegal trade there, which made up a huge chunk of the local economy. They were famous for their chop shops.

Which explained their interest in Riley. If you build your business on the quick turnover of hot wheels, it's to your benefit to employ a guy who can boost a car and leave the music playing.

The Bottom Boys were small-time, but they thought they were ferocious. Like any street gang, they could be dangerous. When I took the job to look for Riley, I hadn't counted on dangerous. I considered heading back to Hyde Pier and taking Heidi up on breakfast. Maybe lunch too.

"Don't worry," I said, patting her hand. It felt like biscuit dough. "I'll find him."

I stood to leave. She struggled to her feet and walked me to the door.

"Riley means well," she said. "He's always wanted to be... more. More handsome. More athletic. More popular. He's never been satisfied to be Riley. He's good to me, you know."

"I'm sure."

"He keeps telling me he'll take care of me. Every day. '*I'm gonna make a lot of money, Ma.*' '*Someday I'm gonna buy you a big house, Ma.*' '*You know, Ma, I'm gonna take you on a cruise to Hawaii.*' '*I'm gonna be a big man, Ma. People are gonna respect me someday.*'. He's full of dreams, Riley. But you know what?"

"What?" I said.

"It's all just talk. He talks big, and he dreams big, but when you get right down to it, Riley's just the King of Gonna."

FIVE

I wasn't happy to discover Riley hanging with the Bottom Boys. I'm a tough guy, though. I can cope.

It helped that one of the gang owed me a favor. Mooch Gomez had hired me a couple of years back to do some divorce work when he suspected his wife was playing around on him. In the course of my investigation, I uncovered a plot by his wife and her boyfriend to kill Mooch and collect his life insurance. When all was said and done, Mooch got his divorce. His wife got to eat state food for a couple dozen years. Mooch told me he was at my disposal if I ever needed a favor.

He answered on the second ring when I called him on my cell. We exchanged pleasantries, and then I waded on in.

"Gordy?" Mooch asked. "Is he in some kind of trouble?"

"No," I said. "Well, no more than usual, I suppose. He's a Bottom Boy, after all."

"So why you need him?"

"He's been seen around town with a guy I'm looking for. I just need to ask if Gordy's seen him the last day or so."

"Gotcha. Fact is, I ain't seen Gordy for a while myself. He used to be in real tight with us, but he's been scarce of late. Who's the guy you're looking for?"

"Fellow named Riley Quinch."

"Cap'n!" Mooch said.

"Pardon."

"We call him Cap'n Quinch. Y'know, like that cereal."

"You've seen him around?"

"Not for weeks. Riley brought in a few cars last month for…uh…body work. Since then, nothin'. Now I think of it, that was about the time we stopped seeing Gordy. Got a pen?"

I fished in my glove compartment.

"Sure," I said.

"Lemme give you the last address I had for Gordy. He might still be there, and then he might not. Couldn't tell you for certain."

I wrote the address on my notepad.

"Is Cap'n in big trouble?" Mooch asked.

"Big enough. I think he's going down on these new charges. He's pretty much worn out any welcome he had in the municipal courts."

"That's not good. Caught between a rock and a hard place, ain't he?"

"What do you mean?"

"Riley screwed up in a big way. He was supposed to deliver a Mercedes SEL about a week ago. He found the car, boosted it, but then he sold it to a shop over in Pacifica instead. Guy I know, kind of guy you don't want to cross, would like to take a piece out of his hide. You didn't hear this from me, but it might be best if you find him real quick. Could save him a major smackdown."

"Thanks," I said. "And, don't let Gordy know I'm coming. Like I said, he's in the clear, but I don't want him to get spooked and rabbit on me."

———————

Maybe Riley was crashing at Gordy Carlton's place, and maybe he wasn't. Carlton was my only solid lead, though, so I set up a stakeout near Gordy's tiny rental house in Hunter's Point. It was a concrete block affair that someone had tried to spruce up with some paint and a useless gable over the front door. There was a bare light bulb hanging on a cord inside the gable. The yard was mostly dirt and discarded beer cans.

A faded Ford sedan with illegal window tints sat in the gravel driveway. I wrote down the tag number, in case I might need it later, and waited.

And waited.

The afternoon wore on. I tried several stations on my satellite radio, looking for something to stave off boredom. After a while I pulled out an e-reader and plowed through a few of the middle chapters of a new author I was reading, but even that became tiresome. I considered setting fire to the house to see who ran out. That seemed extreme, so I waited some more.

Finally, around seven that evening, the front door opened. A guy matching Gordy's description—short, dumpy, wearing a Bottom Boys tee shirt, and carrying enough metal in his face to build a Volkswagen—walked out to the Ford and drove away.

Having nothing more productive to do, I followed him.

He drove toward Bayview, an area of the city only slightly more palatable than Hunter's Point. I kept a couple of cars between us and tried not to do anything flashy that would draw attention to myself. I don't think it would have mattered. From what I had seen and heard about Gordy Carlton, he was pretty oblivious to anything you couldn't eat, drink, or screw. Tradecraft is a point of pride in my business, though, so I kept it surreptitious.

He parked on Third Street and walked into a bar. It was dark by then, and I could see him through the front windows. He perched on a stool and ordered a bottle of beer. A couple of guys were playing pool in a corner, and there was a football game on the ancient TV suspended over the bar. Gordy looked like he was settled in for a while, so I stepped into a pizza shack across the street and bought a couple of slices of garbage pie and a big soda, keeping an eye on the bar the entire time.

I didn't have any guarantees that Riley would show up. On the other hand, if his mother was correct and Riley and Gordy were tight, sooner or later I'd see them together.

One in the morning, and I still lounged in the front seat of my car watching people slouch their way out of the nightclub, waiting for Riley to show his face. People came and people went, but Carlton stayed planted at the bar, knocking back longneck beers and watching the tube. He played a game or two of pool. Either he really loved the seedy joint, or he was waiting for someone.

It seemed as if I spent half my life sitting outside bars, motels, trailer parks, apartments, and even the occasional library, staring at the door and listening to public radio through my earbuds, or reading an e-book, or just wool gathering about the way I'd mismanaged my life to this point.

19

It isn't a good idea to let your mind wander too far. After an hour or two of serious navel-gazing, I started to think about heavy shit like destiny and mortality and the nature of the universe. There must have been a reason why I was a by-the-hour private cop, and not a surgeon or a tycoon or a politician. I searched my memory for clues, hoping it wasn't because of some stupid spur-of-the-moment "Hey, y'all, watch this!" impulse that bent my trunk and steered me on my life trajectory. Because, if it was all my fault, I owed myself a lot of apologies.

Thinking shit like that can keep a guy awake, which is a plus in my profession. It's hell on your peace of mind, though.

One-thirty rolled around, and no Riley Quinch. The bartender would have made last call. It was a matter of time.

A guy wearing a windbreaker and a golf cap walked out of the bar. He looked thirty-five or forty. On his arm was a young woman, certainly no more than twenty and probably carrying a fake ID. They turned right and walked toward a bank teller machine halfway down the block. The girl wobbled on three-inch heels and wore a glittery dress she probably thought made her look sophisticated, but really advertised her as a mark.

I had seen this game before.

The man headed straight for the teller machine.

"*Hold on honey,*" I narrated, as they reached it, "*I gotta get some money so we can have us a real party.*"

They walked right past the machine. For a second, I felt like I had lost a bet. I shrugged my shoulders.

"It's all right with me," I said.

Then the man stopped. He looked back at the machine and pointed. The girl nodded like a bobblehead. The guy slipped his card into the machine. Seconds later he pulled his card out and turned back to the girl. He jerked a thumb back at the machine and shrugged.

"*Well, shoot, honey,*" I said affecting a good ol' boy accent, "*Looks like my paycheck hasn't cleared yet. Guess I can't afford that party after all. I'll just see you home.*"

The girl pouted and then smiled. She held up her purse and gestured toward the machine.

"*No problem,*" I said in a bad falsetto. "*I can get some money, and you can pay me back later.*"

The man rubbed his face, and then he waved his hands in front of him, and he shook his head.

"*I couldn't let you. It wouldn't be right. I'll just take you home and we'll get together some other time,*" I said.

The girl placed one hand on the man's shoulder, and then walked unsteadily past him to the teller machine.

"*No, really!*" I said. "*It's no problem, and it's early yet!*"

I knew what was coming. She'd give him the money. He'd walk a block or two with her, until nobody was in sight, and then he'd push her into a pile of garbage bags and take off running. It was one of the oldest short cons in the book, but it works like a charm on young women with daddy issues.

And that's the way it went down. At least the first part. The girl gave him whatever cash she got from the machine, put her arm inside his, and they headed down the sidewalk toward the next block.

It was none of my business. Gullible people get ripped off all the time in this world. Some people think victims deserve it for trusting people who are clearly untrustworthy. Some people think marks need to be taken advantage of occasionally, so they can learn how the world works.

I'm not some people.

I hopped from my car and trotted after them. I knew the neighborhood. The part we were in was the kind of place the tourist boards tell you to avoid after sunset. Where they were headed was worse.

I caught up with them about a block and a half away. I heard the guy say, "This is an after-hours place. Not completely legit, you know? The entrance is off this alley."

I know about every after-hours bar in town. This wasn't one of them.

He steered her right when they reached the gap in the buildings. I walked up right behind the guy and stuck the barrel of my Browning in the middle of his spine.

"Stop," I said.

He froze. The girl turned around. She saw the gun and pulled closer to the man.

"*Oh God Oh God Oh God!*" she cried.

"Relax," I told her. "I'm not robbing you."

She looked at me the way a cat would stare at an abacus, curious but with a complete lack of understanding.

"You aren't?"

"No, but *he* is," I said, as I slapped the back of the man's head. "You just met him in that bar tonight?"

She nodded, her eyes like huge obsidian saucers.

"He's running a con on you. How much money did you get out of the machine?"

"A...a hundred," she stammered.

I pushed the pistol harder into the guy's backbone.

"Give it back," I said.

He pulled the money from his jacket pocket and handed it to her.

"Go home," I told her. "Think about what almost happened here tonight. Get your shit together. Go to community college, become a dental hygienist or something, and stay away from this part of town."

She nodded some more but kept staring at me.

"Go!" I yelled, and the spell was broken. She backed out of the alley, turned, and started to jog unsteadily away. I waited until I couldn't hear her heels clicking the concrete.

"What about me?" the guy said.

"Hold up your license."

He dug his wallet from his pocket and held it up.

"Turn around," I said

He did. I pushed him back against the bricks and speared his breastbone with the pistol. I yanked out my phone and shot a picture of the license.

"Put it back. Do you have any idea who that girl was?"

"N-no," he said, his eyes riveted on the steel jammed against his sternum.

"She. Is. Protected. Got that?"

"Yeah. Sure. I ever see her again, I'll head the other way. Whatever. Just put the gun away."

"I see you hustling young girls on the street again, you'll get to see what a week in the hospital feels like. Do we understand one another?"

He nodded, without taking his eyes off the gun. He looked a little green. For a second, I thought he might ralph all over my Skechers.

"Take a hike," I said. "Make it a long one. Get lost."

I waved him away with the gun, and he took off in the same direction the girl had fled.

"Hey!" I shouted. He froze and looked back at me. "Uh-uh. Wrong direction."

He turned and dashed back by me. I gave him a ten-count. Then I left the alley and headed back toward the bar. I didn't see Carlton through the window anymore. I walked inside. The music was off, and one of the bartenders was clearing the taps. I got his attention.

"There was a guy here in a brown leather jacket, wearing about ten pounds of jewelry," I said.

"You mean Carlton?" the guy said.

"That's him."

"He left. Maybe ten minutes ago."

I pulled Riley Quinch's picture from my jacket.

"You know this guy?"

"No, but he was just here. Bopped in just before Carlton left. They took off together."

And that was how my night went. Riley was in the wind again, and I was wiped out. I decided to call it a day, head to Heidi's place for a few hours, and get a fresh start in the morning.

One problem. My car was missing.

"Damn it, Riley!" I cursed.

At least I'd saved a damsel in distress.

I wondered whether Superman ever had days like mine.

SIX

I could have tried calling a cab or an Uber, but there was no way they were going to drive out to Bayview after midnight to rescue my stupid ass. I tried to recall whether I'd locked my door when I left to save the girl from her con man predator, and then I decided that it didn't matter. Locks are minor annoyances for a pro like Riley.

Heidi sounded groggy when she picked up the phone.

"*Wha...?*" she mumbled.

"It's Eamon," I said.

"Don't have to call first, baby. You got a key. Come on over."

I explained my predicament, and she woke right up.

"I'll be there in half an hour," she said.

It took almost forty-five minutes, but it was worth it when she finally pulled up in front of the bar. She looked like she'd showered and preened. Next to her, after my day-long stakeout, I looked like a hobo.

"So, your skip made off with your car?" she asked, not trying to hide her amusement.

"We shall never speak of this again," I said.

"The hell we won't. I'm riding this for weeks."

"I was going to take you to Santa Catalina Island with the money from this job."

She thought about it. "Got it. Lips sealed. Want to file a police report?"

"Not yet. Take me to Hunter's Point."

"Why don't I just rape and kill myself here and save the gas?"

"You'll be okay. If I'm right, I know where the car is."

A few minutes later, we pulled up in front of Gordy Carlton's brick shack. Sure enough, my car sat out front. Gordy's was missing.

I checked my Browning and leaned over to kiss Heidi.

"Lock the doors and head on home," I said. "I'll call you in the morning."

"What are you going to do?"

"First, I'm getting my car back. Then I'm going to find out where Riley is laying his head. Don't worry. I'll be fine."

I kissed her again, with a promise for more, and she headed back toward her place on Russian Hill. After her taillights turned at the end of the street, I banged on Gordy's front door. He opened it. I shoved the Browning in his face.

"Inside," I said.

He didn't argue. I backed him into the house, and immediately regretted it. The place smelled like old cheese wrapped in a towel soaked in ranch dressing and left in a car in the desert for a week. My nose wrinkled, and I felt like gagging. I forced it back.

"Where's Riley?" I said.

"Don't know, dude. Who in hell are you?"

I flashed him my badge and license. "You were in a bar over on Third Street in Bayview this evening with Riley Quinch. Don't deny it."

"Why would I? Sure. I was with Riley. We came back here, smoked a jay, and then he took off. End of story."

"You gave him your car?"

"What?" Gordy yelped. He pushed past me, heading for the door. I tripped him, and he yowled as he fell face first toward the stained carpet. He could see through the open door, though, and he beat the floor with his fist in anger.

"Damn it! Can't trust nobody no more!"

"He stole your car, too," I said.

"When I get my hands on him..."

"Don't count on it happening soon. Riley's in big legal trouble, and if you've been helping him you could be charged with harboring a fugitive."

"Shit, man. I don't need that sort of hassle."

"Then tell me where he is."

Gordy pulled himself off the floor and walked back over to the couch.

"I don't know. He called me earlier today, wanted to meet with me to help him get some more business with the Bottom Boys chop shops. Dude's crazy. The Bottom Boys want to toss him into a car crusher right now. All he told me is he's been hanging out over in the Tenderloin."

"No address?"

"Just the Tenderloin. That's all I know."

I holstered the Browning. I'd only used it for effect anyway. Any day I couldn't take a punk like Gordy, I'd hand in my license.

"Don't tell him I was here," I said. "If I find out you've tipped him off, I'll be back. You don't want me to come back."

"Don't worry, man. Riley better hope you find him before I do."

SEVEN

The next afternoon, I cruised SoMa in my recovered car. I was sick and tired of chasing Riley all over town, so I had a pair of cuffs on my belt, some manacles in the trunk in case Riley got the rabbit habit, and a double-shot Taser X2 under the front seat.

It was a gorgeous day in San Francisco, which was a nice change after two straight weeks of clouds and cold drizzle.

Riley Quinch had two weaknesses—cars and Baskin-Robbins German Chocolate Cake ice cream. I figured, if he was hanging down in the Tenderloin, sooner or later he'd come out of his hole for a goodie.

I sat in my car in a parking lot across from the Baskin-Robbins on Mission, listening to a Giants businessman's special game against the Braves. It was late in the season, right before the playoffs. The Braves had just scored a go-ahead run when I saw Riley juke up the sidewalk toward the ice cream store. He wasn't terribly tall, but his gaunt, scarecrow-like frame made him look lanky and loose as he walked, flinging apparently boneless arms back and forth in time to some melody only he could hear.

As I had expected, he ducked into the Baskin Robbins. I could see him through the glass, as he ordered a double cup of his favorite. I allowed him to sit before I crossed the street to follow him in.

"Riley," I said, nodding at him as I walked in and headed for the counter.

"Hiya, Mr. Gold," he said, just before shoveling a huge gob of ice cream into his mouth.

I flashed the counter server my license and pushed one of my cards across the glass.

"I'm a private detective and a bounty hunter," I told him. "That guy giving himself brain freeze jumped bail on a felony car boosting beef. I'm going to arrest him. You cool with that?"

The counter server glanced at Riley and then back at me.

"Just don't bust up the place, okay?"

"Sure. Gimme a cone of butter pecan."

He handed me the cone and I crossed to the booth where Riley was sitting. I slid into the seat across from him.

"Guess I fucked up, huh?" he said, between bites.

"Yeah, you kind of did," I said.

"I didn't mean to, Mr. Gold. I don't know what happened. I knew I had that court hearing, but then one thing after another went down, and the next thing I knew I'd missed it."

I ate some of my ice cream.

"You know, dude," I said, after swallowing, "your mother staked her house to make your bond."

"Yeah. But I knew Doogie wouldn't drop on her. He's been like one of her adopted kids since he was five or six."

"You might be counting just a little too heavily on Doogie's sentimentality. He's pretty pissed right now. He might just take your mom's house and charge her rent to live there."

"I don't think he'd do that."

"What do you say we don't test it?" I said.

"Okay."

I looked closely at his head.

"Hey, you doing the hair club thing, Riley? It looks like you have some new growth going on up there."

He smiled and blushed a little.

"Naw, man, I can't afford that shit. This is just a little weave. They take real hair, like, and they tie it in knots with your natural hair. It thickens things up."

"No kidding? What's something like that cost?"

"A coupla bills for me, on account of I don't got so much real hair, you know?"

He had eaten every bit of the ice cream he could get with a spoon, so he finished it off by licking around the inside of the cup. He stood and tossed the cup and the plastic spoon into the trash can.

"You have to use the cuffs?" he asked.

"I don't know, Riley. Do I?"

"I don't reckon, Mr. Gold."

I finished my cone and wiped my hands on the midget napkins the store kept at the tables.

"Can I get a cup to go?" he asked. "From what Doogie tol' me, I might not get any for a while."

"You aren't going to smear it all over my seats?"

"No sir."

"Sure, then. Knock yourself out."

He bought another cup of German Chocolate Cake and walked with me out to my car. I held the passenger door for him, and he slid into the front seat. After locking the door, I walked around and climbed behind the wheel.

We had driven about two blocks when Riley spoke again.

"Can you do something for me?" he asked.

"Depends."

"If I give you my mother's telephone number, would you call her and tell her I'm in the slam?"

"Did you really just say *in the slam*?"

"Huh?"

"Never mind. Sure. I'll tell her."

"You got something to write with?"

I pulled the car over to the curb next to a small park and killed the engine. I fished around in the glove compartment for a notepad, dug a plastic ballpoint from my shirt pocket, and handed them to him.

Riley started to write a number on the pad. Then he turned the pen around and jabbed the ballpoint into the meat of my right thigh.

As I stared at the pen protruding from my leg, Riley jerked open the passenger door and jumped out.

He got about twenty feet before I drew a bullseye on his backside through the open door with the Taser. He obviously thought he'd been shot with double ought. He jumped about two feet in the air and twisted as he fell to the grass, twitching as he rolled around. His trousers darkened as he lost muscular control.

"*Oh my god oh my god oh my god you shot me!*" he wailed, as the shock wore off.

I gingerly extricated myself from the car, being careful to avoid hitting the pen which was still stuck in my thigh. I had heard it was a bad idea to pull an impaled object from your body. It might be plugging up something you don't want unplugged.

I limped over to Riley, who was still rolling on the grass, his hands cradling his butt. I gave him a second jolt just to make sure he knew I meant business. I stuck my foot into the small of his back and cuffed him. "Damn it, Riley, look what you did," I said, pointing to my leg. "Now I have to explain to your mom why I had to shoot you in the ass."

I made Riley lie on his stomach in the back seat of the car. He'd shit his pants pretty bad, and I knew who would have to get that out of my upholstery. I drove to the hospital, where I parked in the ER lot.

I limped into the waiting area, and stood for several seconds at the nursing station, trying to get someone's attention.

Finally, a student nurse looked over at me. I think she gasped.

"Sir, you have a ballpoint pen stuck in your leg," she said. I nodded.

"I also have a guy with a couple of Taser barbs in his ass lying in the back of my car," I told her. "I think you'll probably need a gurney for him, unless you want to sacrifice a wheelchair. And don't take off the handcuffs."

She stared at me for a moment. This was, apparently, a new medical experience for her.

"I'll get a doctor," she said.

Riley and I were placed in adjoining exam bays. I asked the nurse to open the curtain.

"I can't believe you shot me," Riley moaned.

"*Hello*," I said, pointing to the pen sticking out of my thigh. "This was a brand-new pair of pants."

"So were these," he said fanning his cuffed hands over the stained backside of his Levis.

A doctor stepped inside the bay and looked us over.

"Impalement beats Taser," he said after a couple of minutes. "You're first."

They wheeled me down to x-ray to make certain Riley hadn't invaded my femoral artery with the pen, and then took me back to the ER. Riley was still there, lying on his stomach, his hands folded peacefully over his ass. He snored softly.

"Why'd you Tase him?" the doctor asked.

"Riley's not a murderer," I said. "He's not even a bad guy, really. He's just queer for cars. Taser's non-lethal, and a hell of a deterrent should we cross paths again."

"I see. Well, we're going to have to take out that pen. We'll give you a couple of stitches and a shot of penicillin with a tetanus booster, and you should be all right. You'll need to walk with a cane for a couple of weeks, and you'll be sore as hell, but you should recover."

"That's a relief."

"Now let's see about this pal of yours," he said, turning to Riley.

A thought occurred to me.

"Hey," I said. "He also said something about head lice. You should probably shave his hair while you're at it, just to be safe."

EIGHT

It was almost dinnertime when I got back to my office on Jefferson Street near the Hyde Pier. I pulled myself carefully from the car. My thigh was still numb from the lidocaine they'd shot into me before pulling out the pen, but I could tell it was already stiffening. The hospital had provided me with a cane. I used it to limp around to the gallery door.

"My God!" Heidi yelped as I hobbled into the gallery. "What happened?"

"Some moke said Andrew Wyeth was a pussy," I said. "What was I supposed to do, let him run off at the mouth like that?"

"Come have a seat. What really happened?"

"Riley Quinch stabbed me with a ballpoint. I trusted the guy. I'll try not to make that mistake again."

"Are you going to be okay?"

"As long as you stay on top. How about you run over to the Wharf and grab us a couple of Dungeness crabs and some clam chowder while I watch the gallery? I'm really not up to climbing the stairs to my office. Might not be able to get back down."

"Of course. You sit there. I'll be right back."

She kissed me, which was far and away the best thing that had happened all day, and dashed out the front door for the food.

It was a slow day at the gallery. I riffled through some old copies of *ArtNews*. I was on the second magazine when a plain-Jane cop car pulled to the curb. Two men got out. I knew one of them from my days in a bubbletop cruiser in the Tenderloin a couple of decades earlier.

They started toward the stairs leading to my office. If I had been smarter, I'd probably have let them go up, find out I wasn't there, and go away. On the other hand, I had already demonstrated this wasn't one of my smart days.

"Hey, I'm in here," I said.

Steve Gaddy craned his neck around to look in the door of the gallery.

"What in hell are you doing in there, Gold?" he asked.

"Getting in touch with my esthetic side. Looking for me?"

They walked into the gallery. Gaddy pointed at the other guy.

"This is Jasper Durante," he said. "Just got his gold shield."

"Congratulations," I said. "I'd stand, but some perp just stuck a ballpoint in my thigh."

"Man, I hate it when that happens," Durante said, as he shook my hand.

"If this is about Riley Quinch, I can explain. He stabbed me before I Tased him. It was self-defense."

Durante glanced over at Gaddy. He looked concerned.

"No, but we can talk about that later," Gaddy said. "Does the name Abner Carlisle mean anything to you?"

"Sure. He came to see me a few days ago. He wanted me to find some guy named Eddie Rice."

"Did you find him yet?"

"Never tried. I turned down the case."

"Why?" Durante asked.

"Because, unlike you guys, I don't have to take every job that comes my way. This one didn't smell right. I had a feeling Carlisle planned to do something violent to Rice, and I didn't want to be a part of that."

"Why did you think that?"

I looked at them for a second. Maybe the lidocaine had migrated to my brain, or maybe I was just on sensory overload. I had missed something critical.

"What's happened?" I asked.

Gaddy sat in the other chair. Durante stayed on his feet.

Gaddy pulled a notepad from his jacket pocket and glanced over it.

"About ten this morning, a maid at a flop in the Tenderloin ignored a *No Moleste* sign on a room door and used her pass key to go in and make the bed. She couldn't, because Abner Carlisle was still in it. She excused herself and started to walk back out, but then she slipped in the pool of blood at the side of the bed and fell on her ass."

"Someone killed him?" I asked.

"Either that or he shot himself in the head four times. It'll be a week before we get any autopsy results, but the crime guys on the scene used liver temp to establish time of death as sometime around eleven last night. We found a cheap datebook in his belongings. There was a note in it about meeting with you last Friday. Thought you might know a thing or two about him."

I rubbed my face and thought about it.

"I'd look for Eddie Rice," I said.

"Suppose you fill us in on the background."

"Carlisle just got out of prison. He was there for almost thirty years for some armored car robbery. He and five other guys were in on it, but only four of them drew any time. They shielded this guy Rice, who was supposed to take care of the stolen money for them until they got out. Problem was, the only one who ever made it out was Carlisle. This Rice character apparently disappeared about twenty-five years ago with Carlisle's daughter."

"Living the high life," Durante said.

"Probably. You can open a lot of bottles of champagne with thirteen million."

"Thirteen million?" Gaddy said. "I think I could kill to protect that kind of stash."

"That's what I was thinking," I said. "Carlisle wanted me to find Eddie Rice. I'm betting Rice found him first."

Gaddy closed the notebook and put it back in his pocket.

"I think maybe you did the right thing turning down this case," he told me. "Maybe saved yourself a lot of hurt. Thanks, Gold. See you around."

Durante said goodbye also, and they both walked back to the car. I watched as they drove up Hyde toward Market.

I thought about it for a few moments, and then picked up Heidi's phone.

Artie Becker answered on the second ring.

"This is Eamon Gold," I said.

"I was just thinking about you," Becker said.

"Your jerkoff fantasies are your business. Did a guy named Abner Carlisle come to see you?"

"How'd you know?"

"Because I referred him to you. He tossed the paper I wrote your name and number on, but he read it pretty closely first. Thought maybe he remembered it and thought better about looking you up later."

"That's real interesting, Gold, considering I sent him to you in the first place."

"Say again?"

"He came to me middle of last week. Told me he was looking for his little girl who ran off with some guy named Eddie Rice."

"Did he tell you why he wanted Rice?"

"You mean the take from the armored car job? Sure. It sounded like a Chinese clusterfuck from the first sentence. I wasn't interested in cluttering my life with it. You like challenges, though, so I sent him to you. You going to take the case after all?"

I thought about it for a second.

"Yeah," I said. "I think maybe I will."

NINE

What the hell?

I was bucks up, and I wasn't going to be hale enough to run down any skips for a couple of weeks. I figured I could spend a little time doing some head work trying to find this Eddie Rice fellow. Of course, there was a lot of information I still didn't have. I was missing some key facts, like the daughter's name. Most of what I didn't have, I could probably get through the databases.

I was still running over the steps I'd have to take when Heidi showed up with a couple of crabs and sourdough bowls of clam chowder.

"Any customers?" she asked, as she set the food on the counter.

"No, but the cops dropped by."

"Do tell? They buy anything?"

Like it happened every day.

"Remember that guy I told you about at the gallery the other night? The case I decided not to take?"

"Sure."

"He got himself murdered."

She shuddered.

"Jesus, Gold. How about next time you ease in on news like that. Felt like someone walked over my grave."

"Sorry. That's why the cops were here. This guy, Carlisle, had my name in a datebook. It turns out he was referred to me by Artie Becker."

"Who?"

"Another private investigator in town. A real shithead, but he's good at what he does. Artie smelled the same foul intent I did, so he referred Carlisle to me."

"Artie must like you."

"About as much as I like him. He was yanking my chain, sending Carlisle to me, telling me a case like Carlisle's wasn't important enough for him. Of course, I referred Carlisle right back to him. That's how we feel about each other."

"So, what's the story? Besides the stuff about the armored car."

"You remember that, huh?"

"I was listening. I always listen when you talk. I keep hoping it will rub off on you." She dipped some crab in drawn butter and chewed.

"The guy Carlisle was looking for ran off with Carlisle's daughter."

"And the money," she mumbled through the food.

"And the money."

"How much money?"

"Thirteen million dollars."

Heidi washed down the crab with some iced tea and nodded.

"I think you have it wrong," she said.

"How so?"

"The guy didn't run off with the money and the girl."

41

"I don't understand."

She smiled.

"Because you aren't a woman, Gold. The girl ran off with money and the man."

I spooned some of the chowder and tried it. It was velvety and creamy and perfect. A lot like Heidi.

"You know," I said, after swallowing. "I think you might be right."

———

Heidi insisted I spend the night at her house that evening, so she could—as she put it—*do a Florence Nightingale* on me. She did something on me, all right, but I'm not certain it was approved by the American Medical Association. She was careful, though, because we didn't want to burst my stitches.

When I woke the next morning, she was already gone. I checked the clock. Ten-fifteen. It was the latest I had slept in months.

I washed, taking care not to get my bandages wet, raided her refrigerator for some breakfast, and then tidied before I locked up.

I bought my Russian Hill house right after a major quake turned the Marina house my parents had left me into a smoldering ruin. The insurance payoff almost took care of the entire cost of my Russian Hill Victorian. Of course, that ol' devil appreciation had worked its magic again in the years since the quake, and I figured if I ever decided to sell the Russian Hill digs, I could afford to buy one or two small Balkan countries.

I took the steps to my front door carefully, because the lidocaine had long since worn off, and my leg hurt like a son of a bitch. I took a few ibuprofens with a pint of orange juice and settled behind my computer.

I am blessed to live in the age of technology. I was in no shape to pound the concrete following up leads on Carlisle's daughter, especially when I had CyberShamus at my disposal. For an extortionate monthly fee, I had access to most of the public records in the United States, and many from Canada.

I powered up the Dell and logged on to CyberShamus. After verifying my status as a Gold Member (which I always found just a little too tritely ironic) I started hunting around.

I started with *armored car robberies California.*

It took me about two minutes to find several accounts of the job Carlisle and his buddies tried to pull off. The newspaper accounts of the time made a big deal about the irony of Officer Walt Petter being on the scene at the time of the robbery, because his police cruiser had run over a broken bottle and sustained a flat tire.

Apparently, the Carlisle gang had plotted out the routes for this particular armored car which made a long, circuitous delivery schedule to the local big box discount stores. They had decided there were two locations on the route that were fairly deserted. Their inside man, Charles Ells, was a dispatcher. Since he had planned to disappear right after the robbery, he figured he could get away with calling the car and telling it to stop at a disabled car to take on the payload while the imaginary second car waited for a service vehicle. Ells made the call, then pretended to come down sick with a stomach virus and left to pick up his bags to meet Carlisle after the job.

Officer Petter blew a tire just half a block from the site Carlisle had chosen, and had the bad luck to do it five minutes after Ells made the call and took his act on the road.

The rest of the story played out like a bad caper film. One thing after another went wrong, and before it was over Prodnow had killed Petter and one of the armored car couriers, and had left the other courier shitting into a bag for the rest of his life.

This was all *before* the local police responded to Petter's call for assistance and arrested the entire group. By that point, the paper said, one or more unknown accomplices had fled with the money while the rest of the gang made a stand against the cops. The money was never recovered. The rest was mostly legal proceedings and long prison sentences.

None of the news articles mentioned Eddie Rice. They were kind enough to provide the ages for each of the felons, which gave me a starting point for locating everything I could find on Abner Carlisle.

I ran a search for Carlisle, using a presumptive birthdate about seventy years ago. The census report produced fifteen hits. I cross-referenced them against canceled Social Security numbers, since the numbers were recycled when someone died. That narrowed my list down to four. I copied their Social Security numbers and ran geographic searches for them. One lived in Omaha, one lived in North Carolina, and a third one lived in Boca Raton, Florida. The fourth listed a last known address as a post office box in Wyoming.

Bingo.

I backed out and ran a new search on Abner Carlisle's social security number. There wasn't a lot to find, since he had been pretty much out of circulation for three decades.

I got date of birth, a record of a marriage to a woman named Joan Page, divorced twenty years later, and a mention of one daughter, born while Abner and Joan lived in Lompoc. The daughter's name was Lydia Frances. My guess was she had been named after one grandmother or another, since this was the height of a period in history when many kids were given names like *Rainbow* and *Electrolux* and *god*.

No other marriages listed, so I presumed the daughter who ran off with Eddie Rice was Lydia Frances Carlisle.

I ran a search on her, got her Social Security number, and checked her history. She would have been sixteen when the robbery went down, which would have made her twenty-ish when Eddie Rice disappeared. There was no reference to her after her twenty-first birthday. It was as if she vanished from the face of the Earth.

As a trained investigator, I knew that this meant one of two things. Either she was dead, and her death hadn't been reported to anyone, or she had put a lot of effort into making herself scarce. It would have entailed changing her name, Social Security number, and other details. As long as she didn't have any fingerprints on record, she could simply melt into the human parade and resurface as virtually anyone she wanted to be.

I tried to locate Eddie Rice. It was a cinch this search would likely come up empty also, but I gave it a shot anyway.

Edward Carl Rice had been born in Modesto, where he had spent most of his early years. A significant portion of those years were passed in one juvenile facility or another. He had been labeled *incorrigible* by the courts by age twelve, and apparently never slept in his widowed mother's house again before reaching his majority.

Surprisingly, he appeared to have reformed by then, as I couldn't find a single reference to a violation after his eighteenth birthday. His record showed him employed at only three businesses between age eighteen and the armored car robbery, so his work history was pretty stable. I wrote down the businesses and moved on.

After that, as I had predicted, nothing. Like Lydia Frances Carlisle, his number dropped off the charts about twenty-five years ago.

I logged off, hobbled into the kitchen for a Killian's, and relaxed on the couch while I thought the whole mess through.

Eddie and Lydia hadn't left much of a trail to sniff. Lydia's father was dead, along with all the other conspirators except for Eddie. Nobody had seen hide nor hair of Eddie and Lydia since four years after the robbery.

I could run down each of the businesses where Eddie worked, but that seemed like a fruitless exercise. America is the land of the mobile workforce, and the likelihood that anyone remained at any of those businesses who remembered anything substantial about him was pretty low.

I picked up the telephone and called the armored car company. After a couple of holds, my call wound up in the office of a man named John Rascoe in Risk Management.

"My name is Eamon Gold," I told him. "I'm a private investigator in San Francisco."

"What can I do for you, Mr. Gold?"

"About thirty years ago, you had an armored car robbed in Sacramento."

"Yes?"

"None of the money was ever recovered."

"That's correct. I recall the case very clearly."

I said. "One of the robbers was just released from the federal prison in Wyoming, and he came to me the other day to find someone for him. He claimed this person disappeared almost twenty-five years ago with the entire take from the robbery."

There was a brief pause.

"That's interesting," he said.

"Then you'll love this. The guy who tried to hire me was murdered night before last."

"Tell me more. No, wait. This wouldn't be Abner Carlisle?"

"As a matter of fact."

"Of course it was. Nobody else is left. This *is* very interesting, Mr. Gold."

I took a sip of the Killian's, and let his interest grow a little.

"Tell me," I said, "What kind of percentage do you guys offer on recovery?"

He laughed.

"I had a feeling you were going to ask that," he said. "I'm afraid my interest in the case is purely academic. We don't sustain that large a loss very often without recovering at least a small portion. Our insurance company paid off before I even came to work here. Our company really isn't interested in recovery at all."

"I see," I said. "On the other hand, it would seem that your insurer is out about thirteen million now."

"*Thirteen* million, you say?"

I felt a small electric tingle at the back of my neck, and it wasn't from the alcohol.

"That was the number I was given."

"Yes. I think I understand. You see, Mr. Gold, and I'm sure you can understand this, we don't always release accurate numbers regarding how much money is stolen in robberies. After this length of time, though, I don't see any harm. The actual take in that particular robbery amounted to something around twenty million dollars."

"Well, I'll be damned."

"You say Mr. Carlisle told you this fellow had run off with thirteen million?"

"That's what he said."

"This is amusing. Honor among thieves, you know. Whoever actually has the money lied to Carlisle about the true amount."

I thought about it for a moment.

"Mr. Rascoe, would you mind telling me which insurance company paid off on the robbery?"

"Of course. It was Great Pacific Liability. I have the name of the case agent somewhere here in my Rolodex."

I heard the plastic squeak as he checked his cards. My mind ran a subtext wondering how many people still used a Rolodex in the digital age.

"Malvern Robbins," he said. "The last number I had for him was…"

He reeled off the telephone number, and I jotted it on the notepad next to my phone.

"I see," I said. "Maybe I'll give ol' Malvern a buzz."

"Please do. And, Mr. Gold, I would really appreciate it if you could give me a call, should you run down this money.

I'd like to know that the case is finally closed. The one that got away, you know?"

"You'll be the first person I dial," I told him.

TEN

As it happened, Malvern Robbins had keeled over about six months earlier. He'd hopped on the elevator car on the seventeenth floor of his office building, probably looking forward to dinner and a drink, but never made it to the lobby. Massive heart attack. The switchboard operator at Great Pacific Liability redirected me to a woman named Lisa Picardy.

I repeated my story, more or less the way I'd told it to Rascoe, except this time I was careful to include the right amount of money.

"Let me get this straight," she said. "This man came to you claiming to be Abner Carlisle, and told you another man had absconded with all the money from the Sacramento robbery?"

"That's right. Absconded. Good word."

"What was this man's name?"

"Come on, now, Ms. Picardy. Either you're new to this game or you think I am."

"I don't know anything about you, Mr. Gold."

"I'll email my credentials after this call."

"What is it you want?"

"I was just wondering how much Great Pacific pays on recovery."

"That's easy. Ten percent."

"Of twenty million."

"Or whatever portion thereof you can recover, providing you can prove it was part of the original proceeds of the robbery."

"What do you care? Any amount you receive gets credited one way or the other, right? Why on earth would I give you—say—ten million in return for one million, when I could just keep the whole wad?"

"Because you are an honest man?"

"Don't count too strongly on my honesty. On the other hand, I'd rather have one million honest dollars than ten million that keeps me looking over my shoulder every five minutes."

"Aptly put, Mr. Gold. Let's leave it at this. If you bring in any portion of this twenty million dollars and tell us to credit it to the payout on the Sacramento robbery, we'll pay a ten percent fee. I would like to see your credentials in any case."

She gave me her email address. I wrote it down and said goodbye.

I had finished the Killian's, but I didn't want another just yet. I hadn't decided whether I was going to be a tough guy and sweat through the pain in my leg, or just give in and take a painkiller. Somehow, I didn't see Sam Spade choking down a fistful of Vicodin just because some small-time hood shanked him with a ballpoint. On the other hand, Spade was fictitious, and the ache in my thigh was all too real.

I scanned a copy of my license and emailed it to Lisa Picardy along with a link to my website.

I tried taking a short nap, but I never really went to sleep. As I dozed, my brain kept working on the problem. I realized not every road to Lydia Frances Carlisle and Eddie Rice had been washed out.

There was still Abner's ex-wife, Joan, and I hadn't checked to see if anyone in Rice's family was still breathing.

I logged back onto CyberShamus, and quickly located Joan Page Carlisle. Her Social Security number revealed activity as recently as three weeks earlier, which was nice to know. I searched public records and discovered that she had remarried, to a man named Jackson Pike. Their current address was in Mill Valley.

I dressed a little more formally than usual and limped down the stairs to my car. I had already discovered I couldn't jump on the brakes suddenly without experiencing a searing pain in my leg, so it was necessary to drive with my left foot instead of my right.

At least my car had an automatic transmission. Clutching would have been entirely too acrobatic.

I programmed Joan Pike's address into my GPS and cruised across the Golden Gate Bridge into the land of the genuinely well-off. Mill Valley in particular had benefited from the attentions of the heavily moneyed, as I had found on my previous errands there.

The Pikes lived on a cul-de-sac in a neighborhood where the home prices started in the low four millions, and where the average lot ran to about two acres. Fortunately, it wasn't a gated community, since I didn't want her to know I was about to pay a visit. The driveway to her house was unbarricaded.

I parked at the walkway to her front door. The house was the sort of transitional design I had come to regard as a California Box. There was no front porch to speak of, the brick was a fairly common reddish-brown, and the windows were mostly vinyl-clad aluminum to hold down on maintenance. It was about as drab a place as you could possibly manage to build for four million.

When I pushed the doorbell button, I heard an electronic version of the first couple of bars of *Witchcraft* echo through the downstairs. The woman who opened the door was in her middle-sixties, but had held up well through the years, probably with no small assistance from her personal trainer and her plastic surgeon.

She was blonde, the way so many California women are. I could just make out a half-millimeter of gray roots in the part of her hair, but I was enough of a gentleman not to stare.

"Joan Pike?" I asked.

"Yes."

Her voice was suspicious.

I fished out my card and handed it to her.

"I'm afraid I have some bad news for you, ma'am," I said. "May I come in?"

She was still staring at my card, but then she looked up at me, and saw my cane. I leaned on it a little harder, trying to look pathetic.

"Oh, please, do come in."

I followed her inside. She gestured toward a sitting room on the left of the foyer, and I took my time getting to a seat.

"Bad news, you said."

I held the cane in front of me with both hands, and I leaned forward.

"It's about Abner Carlisle," I said. "I'm afraid he's dead, ma'am."

I don't know what I expected from her. Some people, you tell them that their ex has bought the farm, and they get all misty and nostalgic and tell you that, deep down, he was an honorable and gentle man, and it was a shame how life had treated him. Some just go numb.

"Finally," she said, with a sigh.

ELEVEN

I waited for more, but it wasn't forthcoming.

"Finally?" I asked.

"Please understand, Mr. Gold. Our marriage was over decades ago. I've remarried, rebuilt my life. Abner never could let go. He wrote me almost weekly from prison for the first ten years he was there. I never wrote back. When we moved here, I didn't send him my new address."

"What did he write, Ms. Pike?"

"Nothing, really. It was mostly about day-to-day activities, people he knew in prison, that kind of thing. I think he had nothing else to do. I didn't read them after a few years. Mostly, when I saw the return address, I just threw them in the trash."

I nodded. I didn't say anything, because I had learned people try to fill a silence, and I already knew everything *I* had to say.

"The divorce was my idea," she continued. "It was inevitable. Abner was a dreamer. He never could just settle down, work hard, build a future. He always wanted the big score, to make it all in one moment of glory. Our life together was one long succession of get-rich-quick schemes."

"Like the robbery," I said.

"His biggest scheme. I found out later he had planned it for months. He thought it was sure-fire."

"It did work," I said. "The money is still missing."

"But he never saw any of it. None of them did. I suppose it's still out there somewhere, hidden away, waiting for someone to claim it. I don't understand, though. How are you involved with Abner? How did he die? In prison?"

"He was released from prison about two weeks ago. He came to me to ask me to find someone. Two days later, he was murdered."

"So, Abner hired you?"

"Not exactly. I turned him down, ma'am. I sent him to another investigator."

"I don't understand…"

"I'm actually looking for Lydia."

If her facelift had allowed it, I think her jaw would have dropped to the floor.

"I beg your pardon?" she asked.

"Lydia, Ms. Pike. I need to locate her. I have a feeling you know where she is."

Up to that point, she had seemed somewhat fragile and reserved. Now, her face iced over, as she stared me down with frigid eyes.

"You've come here for nothing, I'm afraid," she said. "I'm very busy. I must ask you to leave."

"Has your daughter contacted you, Ms. Pike?"

"Must I call the police?"

"If I'm right, your daughter is involved with the secret fifth conspirator in the armored car robbery. She ran off with him and hasn't been heard from in over twenty-five years."

She looked horrified.

"Except by you, I'd bet," I added.

"Please leave," she said.

"Gladly. Suddenly I feel about as welcome around here as a bad haircut. Just let me know whether you've heard from your daughter."

"I'll answer that," a man said from the foyer.

He was about my height, but considerably older. His head was almost bald, with a wreath of fringy, wispy hair that fell around his ears almost in compensation. His face was leathery, the way you can only get from years working in the sun, tanned deeply behind a thick shock-white mustache.

"I'm Jack Pike," he said. "Please excuse me if I don't shake your hand, but you seem to have upset my wife."

"You handle this," Joan said. She rushed from the room. I heard her sandals clicking rapidly down the hall toward the back of the house.

Jack Pike didn't sit. He stood in the archway of the foyer and stared at me.

"What kind of man are you?" he asked.

I handed him my card.

"A private detective? Who are you working for?"

"For myself. Sometimes people hire me, but even then I work for myself. In this case, Abner Carlisle tried to hire me to find his daughter."

"You mean to find the money."

"That too."

"I overheard most of the conversation. You said Carlisle's dead."

"Also true."

"Which leaves you without a client. Why are you here?"

"Curiosity mostly. That, and the insurance company who paid off on the robbery has offered ten percent on whatever portion of the loot can be recovered."

"You are a bottom feeder, Mr. Gold."

"You say that like it's a bad thing. My gustatory habits notwithstanding, I believe you said you'd answer my question about Lydia."

"Pretty bold for a cripple, aren't you?"

"I have my moments, and this is just a temporary infirmity. If you'd like, I can come back after I heal so you can kick my ass."

He smiled at that one. Then he chuckled a little.

Then he sat down on the couch next to me.

"Yeah, you're tough enough. I knew a lot of fellows like you, back in my wildcatting days. That's how I got all this," he said, waving his hand about. "The oil business used to be full of roughnecks like you. It's nice to know there are still one or two left."

"I know this is an imposition, but the fact remains—whatever Abner Carlisle was looking for got him killed. Whoever killed him is still out there. That's unfinished business."

"Like the armored car money?"

"More unfinished business. Have you heard from Lydia, Mr. Pike?"

He shook his head.

"I've never heard from her. I only married Lydia's mother seven years ago. I've heard all about Lydia, though. It was like she dropped off the face of the earth. She sent Joan a letter, saying she was planning to move to another state. She didn't say which one, only that she'd contact Joan once she settled in."

"Did she mention a man named Eddie Rice in that letter?"

"You mean the guy Abner Carlisle's been harping on ever since he went into the prison?"

"He's spoken with you about Rice?"

"Not with me. In the letters to Joan. He said, someday, this man Rice would show up with a surprise for Joan and Lydia. He never did, of course."

"I think Lydia ran off with Rice," I said. "Rice was the fifth man in the armored car robbery. The other four shielded him, so he could hide the money for them to split once they got out of prison. I've done some tracking on both Rice and your stepdaughter. Neither of their Social Security numbers has been reported to the government as terminated due to death. They just seem to have ceased to exist around 1989, at almost the same moment. If your wife had heard from Lydia since then, it could be a place to start finding her."

Pike stood, his face solemn.

"I wish we could help you, Mr. Gold, but I'm afraid we haven't had any contact at all with Lydia. When she didn't make contact after several weeks, Joan alerted the police. They tried to find her at the time, without any success."

"I beg your pardon, sir, but often the police aren't the best resource to use in a missing person case. They just don't have the manpower to give each case a proper amount of attention."

"That's why we hired a private detective right after I married Joan to help find her. Cost us almost fifteen thousand before he suggested we were wasting our money."

"He came up completely blank."

"Couldn't find a thing. It had been quite some time since Lydia had disappeared, and the detective said the trail was just too cold to follow."

"Did he provide you with a complete report of his investigation?"

"Of course."

"Do you still have it?"

"I think I can lay my hands on it."

"Would you mind giving me a copy when you do? It could save me a lot of legwork if I don't have to retrace steps someone already took without success."

Pike crossed his arms and scowled a little.

"You're really going to pursue this? Even after you saw how it affected my wife?"

"It's what I do. I find things."

"This isn't just about the money?"

"That's part of it, sure. I have to eat like everyone else. Carlisle seemed particularly interested in finding Rice, but he also seemed desperate to find his daughter. I sent him away, because I thought he was planning to kill Rice, and I didn't want to be a part of that. Now I think, maybe, if I'd taken the case, he might still be alive."

"You could have kept him from getting killed."

"I've done it before. Maybe I could have, maybe not, but now he's dead and I feel like maybe I shouldn't have sent him away so quickly."

He stared at me, like some kind of human lie detector, waiting for any sign that I was bullshitting him.

"Sit tight for a second," he said.

I waited as he strode down the hall. I could hear a muffled conversation at the back of the house. Part of it started out animated, but after a few seconds they toned down, and a couple of minutes later Pike reappeared in the archway to the sitting room.

"My wife is still too upset to join us. She did, however, permit me to give you this."

He handed me a picture.

"This is Lydia?" I said.

"Yes. The last picture taken of her before she disappeared. She was about nineteen. It's a school portrait."

"School?"

"UC Berkeley. She attended a couple of years, and then dropped out."

"Did she say why she left?"

"Typical stuff. She was young, she'd been in school for fourteen years, she wanted a taste of life. I didn't know Joan at the time, but as I hear it, she figured Lydia was young enough to do something stupid without suffering really dire consequences in the long term."

I didn't say anything.

"Yes, I know," he said. "Maybe she thinks *she* made too hasty a decision also. Take it, Mr. Gold. We have plenty. The private investigator we hired had them printed. I'll find his report and send it to you."

I struggled to my feet.

"Thank you, Mr. Pike," I said. "I hope I can help."

"So do we," he said, and he showed me to the door.

TWELVE

Pike had hired a guy from Sacramento named Carter to find Lydia. I didn't know Carter personally, but I'd heard his reputation. He was supposed to be competent, and fair to his clients, but not particularly imaginative or exceptionally bright. If Carter told Jackson Pike that looking for Lydia was a waste of time, it was a good bet that he'd only come to that conclusion after giving the search a game try.

His report was well-written and detailed his search efforts. He'd used many of the electronic resources I'd already tried, though seven years earlier the databases hadn't been quite as robust. Even so, he came to the same conclusions. Either Lydia was dead, or she had completely swapped identities.

He had spoken with all of Lydia's friends at Berkeley at the time she disappeared. None of them had heard from the missing girl in years. I made a note in the margin and kept reading.

I needn't have wasted my time. Nothing else jumped out at me. Carter had earned his fifteen grand. I wasn't certain he had done any better than I could, given the trail was colder than the stare of a Catholic school nun when he picked it up. It had chilled for another seven years before Abner Carlisle showed at my door.

It was the weekend. I decided to spend it at my Montara Beach house. Montara is a small community south of Pacifica, right on the PCH, with a decent view of the ocean. I received the house as settlement on a contract with my partner when we started out. He promised me a percentage of the business, but when he stroked out and keeled over into his vichyssoise, I discovered he had raided the accounts to pay back debts. A contract is a contract, and I negotiated with his estate for my due. All he had was a run-down two-bedroom beach house at Montara. Times being what they were, I took it, intending to sell it. As soon as I walked in, I realized it was a keeper.

For a number of years, I've indulged my hobby of woodworking there. I build stringed musical instruments— guitars, dulcimers, Irish harps, and the like. People tell me I'm pretty good at it. I never sell them, because then it would become work. I give some away, donate others to charity auctions and the like, and write off the expenses as publicity. The rest hang on the walls of my Montara house, the living room of which serves as my workshop.

Heidi had joined me for the weekend. We had dinner at the Chart House on Friday, tested the tensile strength of the bed springs for a good part of the night, and lazed around the house the next morning before heading for the beach. It was late September, but unseasonably warm. Sometime between our arrival on the beach and my third beer, she doffed the top of her swimsuit and let the girls out for air. I was always surprised she didn't draw a crowd of oglers when she did this, but this is California, so it probably isn't such a sensation.

I handed her a beer from the cooler we'd brought from the house. She finished slathering on sunblock, for the third or fourth time of the day. Her Northern European skin would fry like a paper-thin slice of halibut if she didn't protect herself. My surfer shorts covered the wound in my leg, but I still hobbled. Relaxing on the beach was more comfortable than surfing anyway.

"I'm working the Abner Carlisle case," I said.

"Who?"

"Creepy really white guy in my office last week."

"Oh, yeah. Thought you decided it wasn't worth the trouble."

"Now it is."

"Some kind of reward money?"

"A little. Ten percent of twenty million if I recover the entire take."

"Not much chance of that," she said.

"How do you figure?"

"It's been thirty years."

"Okay."

"I bet that money went back into circulation years ago. I doubt there's a penny left."

"Only one way to find out," I said.

"Fifty dollars says you come up empty."

"You don't seem certain, wagering only fifty dollars."

"You find the money, I'll give you fifty and I'll do that thing you like so much."

"Seems to me you're pretty fond of it, too."

"So it won't be so bad if I lose."

"No," I said. "It won't."

"What kind of leads do you have?"

"Almost none. I talked with the missing girl's mother the other day. On Monday, I'm meeting with the detective who investigated the robbery. I'm tracking down Eddie Rice's mother. Basic stuff, so far."

"Sure you aren't just looking into this to fill time until your leg heals?"

"Idle hands are the devil's workshop."

"Ah," she said. "Explains why they were so busy last night."

THIRTEEN

Ellis Rhys was the detective who drew the Sacramento armored car robbery. A quick search revealed he was still living, though retired, and had moved to Sausalito. Driving to Sausalito was an immense improvement over making the haul to Sacramento. I called before I left, told him what I was doing, and he invited me to meet him for lunch. My treat.

We met at an Italian place called Poggio on the waterfront. He was waiting for me in the foyer when I walked in. I'd told him I'd be the dark-haired gimp in his late forties with a cane, and he recognized me immediately. He was in his eighties, but still active and vital, with a barrel chest, a full head of shock-white hair, and slightly rheumy blue eyes. His cheeks were flushed, and his nose checked with burst veins. He looked like he could still go two or three rounds with a man half his age.

We took a table next to a window overlooking the bay. Ellis ordered a small plate of carpaccio with truffle pecorino, ramps, arugula, and fried shallots for us to share while we foraged the menu for an entrée. He had good taste. The slivers of filet were buttery and savory. When the waiter returned, I ordered *linguine al vongole*. Ellis ordered *bucatini carbonara*. We decided to split a bottle of chianti. Since I was a San Francisco cop before going private, we passed the first glasses dipping bread in seasoned EVOO and swapping war stories about the job. As I poured the second round, he got around to talking about the matter at hand.

"Sure," he said. "I remember everything about the robbery. Got the call from dispatch while the gunfight was still going down. Hustled to the scene, but by then the perps were sitting on the ground next to the truck in cuffs. Nobody but Wally Petter was killed. Hell, none of the bad guys even took a bullet."

"The newspaper said his name was Walt."

"Maybe his mother called him that. Beats me. I always knew him as Wally."

"You were acquainted with him?"

"I was his training officer when he graduated from the academy. We patrolled in a black and white for his first six months on the job."

"Must have been tough, seeing him go the way he did."

"Took all I had not to execute the bastards who killed him on the spot. Wally was a good kid. He'd been a cop for almost ten years, had trained his own share of rookies. Many of them served as his pallbearers. You say the last of the robbers is dead?"

"A few days ago. He was murdered."

"Should have happened thirty years ago. I hope grass never grows on his grave from all the people who piss on it. I know I'll do my part, if I can squeeze anything past this football of a prostate."

Ellis tore off a piece of the bread and dredged it around the oil before popping it in his mouth.

"Wally was supposed to have a partner the day he died," he continued. "Guy called in sick, and there weren't enough people on the rotation to replace him. No biggie. Patrolmen frequently ride alone. If his partner had been there, Wally might have lived."

"What happened?"

"Dumb fucking luck, that's what. Wally took a short cut down a side street and ran over some broken bottles tossed out by bums. Had a flat left front tire. While he was changing it, the robbery went down a block away. Nobody knows exactly what happened after that, except Wally never called in for backup. SOP says he should have stayed put until reserves arrived, but that wasn't the kind of guy Wally was. He probably decided to take down the robbers using the element of surprise. Instead, he took two in the chest and one in the thigh. The one in the thigh killed him. Severed the femoral artery. He tried to tie it off with his belt, but the wound was too close to his groin. There was no way to stanch the bleeding. He was gone a minute or so after he was hit."

"The man who visited me last week…" I said.

"Abner Carlisle," Ellis said, bitterly.

"Yes. He claimed one of the gang made off with the money."

"Yeah, I heard the story about the missing accomplice too. I know we never saw any of it. It was long gone by the time I arrived. It makes sense someone took off with it. Tell you the truth, Mr. Gold, I never gave two fucks about the money. It was insured. I lost a pal I couldn't replace."

"Carlisle told me the wheelman's name was Eddie Rice."

"Never heard the name. Not in connection with the robbery, or anywhere else for that matter."

"He had a hefty juvie jacket, but no adult convictions or arrests I could find."

"Makes sense. If he had an adult record in Sacramento, I'd have heard of him, and I'd remember. Mind like a steel trap. Faces and names from forty years ago still keep me awake at night."

The waiter arrived with our entrees. They were worth the wait. My linguine was peppered with sautéed clams oozing garlic, white wine, and butter. The pasta was perfectly *al dente*. I filed Poggia away for a visit some other time with Heidi. For a bit, we enjoyed our dishes instead of talking about ancient crimes. Finally, Ellis refreshed his glass with wine and set his fork down.

"Break point," he said. "If I eat any more, there won't be any leftovers. If I take another bite, I gotta finish it, and I'm planning on having it for dinner tomorrow night. One thing about Italian. It only gets better as it sits."

FOURTEEN

My foray to Sausalito took more out of me than I had expected. After making my way back across the bay, I stripped, collapsed into bed, and took a long nap.

I woke around six, immensely refreshed. I remembered Heidi had her ~~drinking~~ book club that evening, so I was on my own. I shoved a frozen deluxe pizza in the oven and popped open a bottle of Anchor Steam before sitting at my computer.

The information on Eddie Rice was sketchy at best. The name was common enough—not exactly Benedict Cumberbatch, you know—so there were myriad opportunities to meander down blind alleys.

I narrowed my search to the correct Eddie Rice just as the oven dinged. I like bubbling the skin off the roof of my mouth about as much as having a Bic pen shoved into my thigh, so I let the pizza cool on the countertop.

Sometimes you find clues in the most unanticipated places. Once I had Eddie's date of birth, I made a run at one of the ancestry sites. It's amazing how much information you can gather from them. According to their records, a person named Edward Rice was born on Eddie's birth date to a woman named Calliope Costanza Rice. Now that was a name that offered little possibility of mistaken identity.

I found Calliope Costanza Rice before the pizza had cooled. Better, she was still alive, though extremely old. Best, she was only a few miles away.

———

I awoke to darkness. Heidi had let herself in and lay next to me, on top of the bedspread, her flaxen hair splayed across the pillow. She snored softly. She looked like Sleeping Beauty. The faint aroma of sauvignon blanc on her breath told me she had come directly from her meeting. I propped up on one elbow. She opened her eyes and smiled at me.

"What time is it?" I asked.

"After ten. How many Vicodin did you take?"

"None. Hate the stuff. Makes me stupid and constipated. I was worn out from a trip to Sausalito."

"Your doctor would disapprove. *I* disapprove. You should be recovering, not galivanting around the bay."

"Working a case," I said, as I rolled over and hopped to the bathroom to brush my teeth.

She ate the rest of the pizza, and we streamed a movie. I don't recall much about the film, but what happened after the end credits was athletic and inventive, at least on her part. One of the benefits of dating a younger woman. Afterward, we lay in bed as the ceiling fan dried the sweat on our bodies.

"How do you find someone who's been missing for almost thirty years?" she asked.

"That's what you were thinking about?"

"Multitasking."

71

"To tell you the truth, I don't think I *will* find her. When all is said and done, I have a feeling I'm going to deliver some bad news to Joan Pike."

FIFTEEN

I'm not sure what I expected, but the Shady Oaks Retirement Home was completely different. I had a vision of a shabby, gloomy, depressing facility where semi-comatose people slouched in wheelchairs, largely ignored by the attendants. I thought it would smell like death and decay.

Instead, I discovered a three-story building that looked very much like a small college. The grounds were meticulously groomed. The lobby looked like I'd just strode into the Mark Hopkins Hotel in San Francisco. Two blue-haired women played a slow but energetic game of ping-pong in a recreation room off to one side of the main desk. I could see an indoor swimming pool down the hall, where a group of saggy men and women engaged in aquatic calisthenics under the watchful direction of a perky woman in her thirties.

I told the woman behind the front desk that I wanted to visit Calliope Rice. Her beaming smile vanished immediately.

"You said Calliope Rice?" she asked.

"Yes."

"Please, wait a minute. I'll let you talk with Mr. Ellroy."

"Who is Mr. Ellroy?"

"He's the facility director. Please have a seat, Mr..."

"Gold." I handed her one of my cards. She glanced at it and her eyes grew wide.

"You're a detective?"

"Private," I said. "Is that a problem?"

"I'll let you discuss it with Mr. Ellroy."

She pointed out a section of functional yet surprisingly comfortable chairs in the lobby and disappeared down a short hallway. Shortly, she returned with a fussy man wearing an expensive pinstripe suit with a yellow power tie. His hair was slicked back with some sort of goo, and he sported a tight, thin mustache. Sizing up people is a stock in trade for guys in my line of work. He looked like the kind of guy the Little Rascals used to torment in their one-reelers. He had an imperious look that suggested a complete lack of tolerance for folderol or humbuggery. People like that irritate me, so I decided not to give him the upper hand. I stood and charged him as politely as possible.

"You're Mr. Ellroy?" I asked, before he could say a word.

"Raymond Ellroy," he said, extending his hand without smiling. I grasped it. It was like shaking with a mannequin. "I understand you would like to visit Calliope Rice."

"That's correct," I said.

"I'm sorry, Mr..." he glanced at the receptionist.

"Gold," she said.

"Yes. I'm sorry, Mr. Gold, but Mrs. Rice seldom receives visitors. This is somewhat irregular. Perhaps you would like to discuss this in my office."

"Is she not permitted visitors?" I asked.

"It isn't that," Ellroy said. "Not at all. It's just...highly irregular."

"So you said."

"Please," he said, gesturing down the hall.

I shrugged and followed him. His office was as pristine and finicky as his haberdashery. His desktop was practically empty, save for a couple of family pictures, a desk calendar, and a telephone with more buttons than a space capsule. A speck of dust would have died of loneliness. He pointed toward a leather wing chair opposite his own office chair. We settled in for a chat.

"May I inquire as to your business with Mrs. Rice?" he asked.

"Why?"

"Beg pardon?"

"The woman, according to you, seldom has any visitors. Perhaps I'm simply an angel of mercy, and my intent is to bring her the comfort of human company to break the monotony of her day."

"I can assure you, monotony is not a problem at Shady Oaks. Our social activities are top shelf. And," he said, as he seemed to survey me from stem to stern, "you don't look much like an angel of mercy to me. More like a thug."

"Judge books by covers much?"

He allowed a smug smile to escape his otherwise stony face. "We deal with all sorts of people here, Mr. Gold. As it happens, we have orders to screen Mrs. Rice's visitors."

"Orders from whom?"

"I don't see where that is germane."

He was digging in. Pushing him would only make him more obstinate. I decided to change the subject. I held up my cane.

"Do you handle rehab cases?"

"It depends. How did you receive your injury, if I might inquire?"

"Bunch of teenagers were harassing some Gray Panthers in the Castro. Couldn't stand by and let them get away with it."

He stared at me. I stared back. I decided not to explain the joke, because then it would be spoiled.

"I only ask because your facility is impressive," I continued. "I've been in a couple of rest homes in my time, but this one takes the cake. Your patients—"

"Residents," he countered. "We don't call them *patients.*"

"Fair enough," I said. "Your residents appear to get the best of everything."

"Thank you," he said, cautiously.

"Not at all what I expected. I suppose this isn't the sort of retirement home you can afford on Medicare and Social Security."

"No," he said. "It isn't. Shady Oaks is more expensive than your typical retirement community, but we also provide a much higher standard of care and a greater variety of life-enhancing activities than your typical assisted care retirement community. While we don't intend to be exclusive, it wouldn't be an exaggeration to say that our residents tend to more affluent, better educated, and generally healthier than average. Actuarially speaking, our residents have a longer life expectancy, and they tend to be healthier and more active later into life. We provide a substantial range of services to make that longer life enjoyable."

"Between you and me, if I wanted to admit my grandmother here, how much would it cost a year?"

"I don't wish to offend, Mr. Gold, but I doubt you could afford it on a..." he glanced at my card. "...private investigator's income."

"You might be surprised. I'm working a case right now that could bring in a couple million dollars for a few days' work. Humor me. How much?"

He told me. It was an impressive number. Zeroes galore.

"I understand why you protect your residents' privacy and confidentiality so fervently," I told him.

"Yes. Our residents demand only the best."

"Admirable. It does beg a question, however. According to my research, Calliope Rice worked for forty years in a middle school cafeteria. She was the lunch lady. She retired on a pension that might buy her a decent meal once a month, and the rest of her income is from Uncle Sugar. I don't suppose you offer sponsorships to the occasional destitute applicant just to avoid accusations of elitism?"

"No," he said. "We do not. What are you implying?"

"This case I'm working," I said. "It involves an armored car robbery about thirty years ago. Mrs. Rice's son was one of the robbers. He disappeared with a substantial amount of money. Between you and me, he's probably dead. He might be alive, though, and if he is alive it could explain how a former middle school lunch lady can afford to live in a posh geriatric palace like Shady Oaks. May I ask who is paying her bills?"

"You may ask," Ellroy said. "But I will not answer."

"But someone *is* paying for her stay here."

"Of course. Someone pays for *everyone's* stay here."

"I don't want to intimidate you. Farthest thing from my mind. In fact, I might be doing you a favor. Are you aware of the penalties in California for receiving stolen property?"

"I'd have no reason to be," he said.

"Perhaps you do. They're impressive. If Eddie Rice is paying for his mother's residence, the money is almost assuredly ill-gotten gains. If I find him, and discover that he's been funding her stay here, you could be implicated by extension."

I watched as the color rose in his face. It had been a good bluff. Fact is, in California, there's a statute of limitations on armed robbery, and it had passed years earlier. Ellroy didn't need to know that.

"On the other hand," I said, "If the money is coming from another source, then you're completely in the clear, right?"

"Look," he said, with a slight stammer, "we don't want any trouble here."

"Neither do I. All I want is a few minutes of Mrs. Rice's time. I promise I won't harass, bullyrag, intimidate, or threaten her. I only want to ask a few questions, and I'll be out of your hair—perhaps permanently."

He weighed his options.

"You said you had orders to screen her visitors," I said. "You've done an admirable job. I obviously intend her no harm. A visit from me might be the high point of her week."

"Yes," he said, drawing out the final consonant like escaping steam. "I see what you mean. Five minutes?"

"Might take ten."

He nodded, picked up the telephone receiver, and punched one of the glowing buttons.

"This is Mr. Ellroy. Could you send someone to escort a visitor to Calliope Rice's room?"

He racked the receiver and faced me again.

"I've never heard of Mrs. Rice's son," he said. "To tell you the truth, I've only met the woman a couple of times. Her bills are paid through a company account belonging to a corporation in San Francisco. Once the financial arrangements were made, I never saw fit to explore them further, as long as the checks arrived the first of each month. They have never been late, though I should note my use of the word 'checks' is somewhat anachronistic. Nobody uses paper anymore, right?"

"Paper is so five years ago."

"Everything is handled as electronic transactions, and I can assure you that Mrs. Rice's accounts are current."

"Good to know," I said. "I don't suppose you'd consider divulging the name of the corporation?"

"What does it matter?"

"I make part of my living uncovering white collar crime. I'm sure you would sleep better knowing the source of a significant portion of Shady Oaks' income is on the up and up."

"You think this man Eddie Rice might be funding her residence through a shell corporation?"

"It wouldn't be the first time it's happened."

"No," he said. "It wouldn't. Let me consider it. Drop back by my office on the way out."

SIXTEEN

Calliope Rice was in her early nineties. She sat in an overstuffed chair placed by a large window in her apartment, which allowed her look out over a neighboring golf course and a heavily wooded glade on the other side. Her eyes were pale and watery behind thick glasses. Her hair was wiry and silver. She had legs like golf bags, with no definition dividing calves from ankles.

Despite her age, she was still in an assisted living apartment. It might have gone three hundred square feet, about the size of a nice hotel room, and equivalently appointed. The bed was homey, with a carved oak frame and a thick crazy quilt bedspread. She had a tiny kitchenette comprised of a refrigerator, sink, and microwave, but no range or oven. I couldn't see inside the bathroom as the attendant ushered me into the room, but I had seen enough of them over the years to know it would be clinical and hospital-like, the only accommodation to infirmity evident in the room, save for a motorized scooter in the corner, plugged into the wall to recharge.

The attendant got her attention and told her she had a visitor. She gazed at me for a long time, as if trying to recall my face. I sat in a chair across from her, and the attendant left us alone in the room.

"Mrs. Rice," I said. "My name is Eamon Gold."

"Have we met?" she asked.

"No ma'am."

"It doesn't matter. It's nice to have visitors."

"You don't see many people?" I asked.

"All dead," she said. "Every one. I had a lot of friends once. One by one, they fell away. I'm the only one left."

"That's a victory of sorts."

"Do you think so? I wonder. Sometimes I sit here and contemplate my funeral. In my imagination, it is a lonely affair. I'm sorry. Have we met?"

I assured her again that we had not. I pulled the picture of Lydia from my jacket pocket and showed it to her.

"Mrs. Rice, do you recognize this woman?"

She donned her reading glasses, which hung around her neck on a gold-filled chain, took the photo in gnarled fingers and stared at it intently. She slowly shook her head.

"I don't know. The face looks familiar. Is she a relative?"

"Her name is Lydia Carlisle," I said. "She disappeared about twenty-five years ago. I think she was with your son, Eddie."

"I see," she said, handing the picture back to me. "I'm old, sir, but I am not addled. You're looking for my son, aren't you?"

"Yes. I am."

"One of many, I'm afraid. When Eddie disappeared, so long ago, men came to see me. They frightened me. They weren't polite like you, but they had the same rough look. They came several times, always in twos. One man would talk. The other would hang back and look menacing. They always asked the same questions. Had I seen Eddie? Had he

81

contacted me? My answer was always the same, and it still is. I haven't seen or heard from my son in over a quarter century. Eventually, they stopped coming. What do you know about Eddie, Mr. Gold?"

"Not a lot. What can you tell me about him?"

"He was a difficult child, almost from birth. He had the colic. Screamed his head off for almost the entire first year. He was a beautiful baby, but he had a temper. He was restless. His father was an over-the-road trucker who died in a huge pileup on an icy highway in Wisconsin on Valentine's Day. Eddie was only four at the time. I took whatever jobs I could to keep a roof over our heads and food on the table. I'm afraid I might have neglected him somewhat in the process. The world is a cruel place for a widow with an unruly child. I cobbled together a mean sort of network of relatives and friends to help keep an eye on him, but he was headstrong. He ran away repeatedly. Got into legal trouble. When he was thirteen, they sent him away."

"The juvenile facility."

"Yes. He spent his teenaged years there. I visited every Sunday. Brought him cookies and cakes. I petitioned the court to release him on his sixteenth birthday, but it was denied. I tried again a year later. The judge seemed adamant that he remained locked up. I spent many years blaming myself for what happened to him. In the end, though, I suppose we're all responsible for ourselves. Do you know what became of my son, Mr. Gold?"

"I'm sorry. I don't. I'm very good at what I do, though, and I will find him."

"When you do, would you be kind enough to let me know? Even if... well, even if he's no longer alive. I would hate to go to my grave without knowing what became of him."

———————

What Calliope Rice had told me was troubling. I had labored under the impression that Eddie Rice was the last remaining member of the crew that heisted the armored car. It was possible the shadowy visitors she had received after Eddie vanished were federal agents, perhaps from Treasury or the FBI. I'd had some experience with those people over the years. They tended to be more buttoned-down attorney and accountant types than thuggish goons, and Calliope had stated the men had frightened her. While intimidation might be part of the repertoire of federal agents, it wasn't their primary approach. They thought themselves too smart to resort to manhandling as an introduction.

The men who had rousted Calliope so many years earlier sounded more like criminals. If so, I might not be the only person still searching for Eddie Rice.

I thanked her for her help and left her to her window on the outside world. I wondered whether she would remember me ten minutes later.

When I arrived at the office downstairs, Ellroy's receptionist said he had been called away a few moments earlier to tend to some crisis elsewhere in the facility, and that I should wait for him in his office when I was finished with Mrs. Rice. She ushered me into Ellroy's office and left me to entertain myself. She did ask whether I'd like a bottle of water or a soda, but I think she was just being polite. I declined.

I checked my email and messages on my phone while I waited. I didn't see the folder on his desk for almost five minutes. It had been left face-side up. I saw the name 'RICE' on the cover.

Ellroy was being cagey. Perhaps he wanted to protect the integrity of Shady Oaks' reputation, or maybe I had scared him with my suggestion that he might be considered an accomplice to the armored car robbery. He knew he couldn't legally release information about the funding of Calliope Rice's residence, but he couldn't stop me from snooping while he was out of the office.

I kept an ear cocked for approaching footsteps, grabbed the folder, and leafed through it. It had tabs for various topics—medical, dietary, recreational activities, and the like. One tab was labeled *Financial.* I thumbed it open and read over the entries.

Part of Calliope's stay was, indeed, paid for by her Medicare and Social Security. She was provided an ample allowance for personal expenses, but the bulk of her entitlement payments went to Shady Oaks. No problem there. It was common for retirement communities to attach public subsidy payments to cover the bills.

The rest of her residence payments—actually, the greater bulk of them—appeared to be from a company called North End Investments. It might have been an annuity, or perhaps Calliope had made some shrewd stock and bond buys over the years and North End Investments was providing the disbursements from an IRA or some sort of 401k.

I closed the file, replaced it on Ellroy's desk, and quickly made my way back to Calliope Rice's room. After knocking politely on the door, I walked in. She was still seated, staring out the window.

"Mrs. Rice?" I asked.

She turned and peered at me.

"Yes?" she asked.

"It's me. Eamon Gold."

"I'm sorry. Have we met?"

I'd seen the phenomenon before. Her short-term memory was shot to hell, but she could recall information from decades earlier in high definition clarity. I decided not to confuse her.

"I'm from Accounting," I said. "I've been looking over your financial records."

"Yes?"

"I just wanted to double-check a couple of things. No problems. I don't want you to worry about anything. I'm just tying up a few loose ends. Are you familiar with a company called North End Investments?"

She looked pensive for a beat or two, and then said, "No. I don't think I am."

"Is it possible you have an investment portfolio of some kind that's partially paying for your expenses here?"

"Oh, my, no. I worked in a school cafeteria. The faculty had a lovely pension program, but we were hourly workers, so we didn't participate. How in the world could I have made investments? I barely survived from one paycheck to another. No. I think you might have me confused with someone else."

"I'm sure that's it," I said. "I'm very sorry to disturb you."

"Think nothing of it. I enjoyed the company. I don't receive many visitors, you know."

I thanked her for her time and returned to the lobby. Ellroy stood at the front desk, chatting with the receptionist. From the way she watched me stride up the hallway in their direction, I think she was warming to me. Ellroy, not so much. He looked like a perturbed undertaker as I reached the desk.

"Did you find what you were looking for, Mr. Gold?" he asked.

"Yes. I think I did," I said.

"Good. Then, we should not expect to see you again?"

It was phrased as a question, but the meaning was clear. Shady Oaks' welcome mat no longer applied to me.

"Not for at least another thirty years or so," I said. "Nice place you have here. I might want to move in someday."

SEVENTEEN

On the way back to my apartment, I called Kevin Krantz through my car's Bluetooth. Apparently, he had caller ID on his phone.

"I knew a guy named Eamon Gold once," he said as a greeting. "Couldn't be you, though. That guy never calls."

I had known Kevin since college. We'd gone in disparate directions in the intervening years. I had become a beat cop and then a detective before handing in my gold shield for a PI's office. He had gone into journalism and had worked his way to the lead business and economics desk at the *Chronicle*.

A few years back, his wife of fifteen years felt a lump in her breast while showering. They say adversity breeds character. Whoever *they* are, Kevin must be their poster child. The hell he went through during his wife's decline can't be imagined, but he bore it with courage, grace, and sometimes even macabre humor. She'd been gone for two years already, but he still wore his wedding ring. He claimed he married for life, and he was still breathing.

I knew a woman once who said there were three levels of friends. When you see Level Three friends across the street, you wave. When you see Level Two friends across the street, you cross the street and spend time with them. When a Level

One friend calls in desperation at two in the morning, you go
to them immediately. Kevin and I are Level One friends.
When his wife died, I was the first person he called after
informing his family. He said he needed a strong back
attached to a weak mind to serve as chief pallbearer. I
accepted before he finished the sentence. We have that sort
of relationship.

"Need some information," I said.

"This about a case, or are you finally going to let me give
you some retirement savings advice?"

"That's funny. Like I'm ever going to retire. Ever hear of
a company called North End Investments?"

"Nope. Why?"

"I'm working sort of a missing person case, guy who
disappeared a quarter century ago. His mother is a resident at
a retirement home that costs way more than she can afford.
Her bills are paid by some outfit called North End
Investments. Funny thing. She never heard of them, says she
has no investment portfolio, and thinks she's living on
Medicare and Social Security."

"And you think your missing person is connected to
North End Investments, paying his mother's bills by proxy."

"Exactly."

"Know anything more about this outfit? Location?
Address?"

"That's why I called you. I figured, if they're legit, you'd
know about them. You already said you never heard of them,
so that answers that question."

"Maybe not. New houses pop up every month, and that
doesn't include the fly-by-night operations. If they handle
money, they're registered somewhere. Wanna make a wager?

I bet they're a shell corporation, acting on behalf of another concern. It may be the only thing they do is pay this woman's bills."

"Think you can run them to ground?"

"Cost you a bottle of Johnny Black and a steak dinner at Alexander's."

"You drive a hard bargain, my friend."

"Bring Heidi along. I miss her face."

EIGHTEEN

It was end of the month. Time to pay bills. I kept all that information at Richmond Street, which meant trudging up the sixteen steps to my second-floor office. The first two steps were a breeze. After that it became a bit of a slog.

I had just finished when someone knocked on my door. Before I could get to my feet, Jackson Pike opened it and walked in.

"Bad time?" he asked.

"Not at all."

He carried a packet, which he placed on my desk as he sat. I was curious, but I figured I could wait for him to tell me what it was.

"Thanks for sending me Mr. Carter's report," I said. "I know he didn't find your stepdaughter, but if it's any consolation he did everything I would have done. He earned his pay."

Pike waved a hand in the air. "I don't care about the money. Money is only a tool. I had a feeling he'd come up empty-handed anyway, but it gave Joan some hope. Are you saying Carter exhausted all avenues to Lydia?"

"No. He only exhausted *his* available avenues. Databases have improved in the last several years. Information has compiled exponentially since then. According to Abner

Carlisle, his daughter probably ran off with this Eddie Rice character. I've located and interviewed Rice's mother. That's more than Carter was able to do, but that isn't his fault."

"That's fascinating," Pike said. "How, um... how did you manage to find her?"

"Like I said, databases are more sophisticated today than they were when Carter worked for you. Plus, I might have a little more imagination. Not to say he's a bad investigator. Not at all. We just approach things differently."

"Yes," he said. "I'll be honest with you, Mr. Gold. When you showed up at our house the other day, I thought you were just another opportunistic fortune hunter. I sent out some feelers since then. Apparently, you're the real deal. Since our last conversation, I've been digging through boxes of records and memorabilia in our attic. I suppose you could say you whetted my curiosity. My wife was devastated when Carter was unable to locate any information on Lydia, but she's doing much better now. I think she had resigned herself to never knowing what became of her daughter. When you appeared, it opened old wounds. I should resent that, but if there's a possibility of putting her mind at ease, I'm willing to work with you. Fact is, I'd like to make this an official investigation."

"It already *is* an official investigation," I said.

"I mean, I'd like you to work for more than just the prospect of a payoff somewhere down the line. I'd like to hire you to find Lydia."

He opened the folder. Paper-clipped to a sheaf of papers was a check.

"A retainer," he continued. "Advance against your billing. Are you working any other cases?"

"No. I should advise you; this could take some time. I'll probably burn through that check in about a week."

"It doesn't matter. There's plenty more where that came from. From what I've heard, if anyone can find Lydia, it's you."

"Buttering me up, Mr. Pike?"

"I only know what my associates have told me. Aubrey Innes was especially enthusiastic in recommending you."

Aubrey Innes ran the cell phone company I'd recently helped. He and I had become friendly during the job. I made a mental note to call and thank him for the referral.

"I don't see a conflict here," I said. "The armored car thing, Eddie Rice, I'm doing on spec for the reward money. Since Rice could lead me to Lydia, I see no reason why I can't do both at the same time."

"Perhaps I can help." He speared the sheaf of papers with a thick index finger. "I found some papers in a box in the attic. Stuff Joan stored away after Lydia was gone for a few years, because looking at it upset her. Lydia was something of a packrat. She never threw anything out. There are some notes in here written by some of her friends in high school, the kind of stuff kids write and drop off in lockers. Perhaps she has been in touch with some of these girls over the years. Also, I found a letter she wrote to a boyfriend. Same deal. Maybe he's heard something."

"It's a long shot," I said. "But who knows? I've started investigations with a lot less. I'll check these out. If you find anything else helpful, you don't have to come all the way into the city to deliver it. Just scan it and email it to the address on my card."

"I needed to see you face-to-face anyway. Joan doesn't know I'm doing this. She's still steamed you showed up unannounced. I don't mind saying you ruined her day. That's not important right now. I didn't tell Joan I planned to hire you, because she's had enough grief. If this works, and you locate Lydia—dead or alive—it will put her mind at ease. Finality, you see. At least she'd know what became of her daughter. If you find nothing, all I've lost is money. I don't want to get her hopes up again if there's a chance it's all a wild goose chase."

NINETEEN

After Pike left, I looked over the papers. They were mostly written in adolescent feminine script, filled with hearts for dots over the 'i's and teenaged polls—*Do you like Ronnie?* with a box for yes and one for no. I have no idea who Ronnie was, but it didn't matter, because Lydia had ticked the *no* box for him. Then she underlined it. Tough for Ronnie.

Most of them were from a girl named Maisie Duncan. As I slogged through the florid declarations of juvenile infatuation, I realized Maisie Duncan and Lydia Carlisle were now approaching their fifties. It was a long shot, but in the age of social media anything is possible, including a woman missing for over twenty-five years contacting an old pal out of the blue.

Since I had her name and probable year of birth, it took me about five minutes to track Maisie down. She'd led an interesting life. Her name was now Maisie Duncan Holloway Sanders Friedlander Pauch. Her current husband, Henry Pauch, was on the San Francisco Board of Supervisors, but legal records suggested they were separated. I found a current address and telephoned her.

"Yes," she said. "Henry and I are separated. A private investigator, you say? Can I hire you to get dirt on him?"

"Perhaps when I find time to breathe. I'm hip deep in a case right now which tangentially involves you."

"How mysterious. What are you doing for dinner, Mr. Gold?"

"I'm eating, but where isn't determined yet."

"Why don't we meet? I'm headed out the door to my Zumba class. Don't have time to talk. Why don't we meet in the bar at the Mark Hopkins? Say, seven o'clock? We can decide where to eat then."

"That's fine. I'll be the deceptively youthful gimp walking with a cane."

It was still hours from my meeting with Maisie, so I studied the box of adolescent detritus Pike had left me. Besides all the notes from Maisie, there was the letter Lydia had written to some boy named Clark Riesenberger. Curiously, she had never posted it. It was folded and slipped into an addressed but unstamped envelope. Having the kid's address—even if it was thirty years ago—was a benefit.

The letter was a laundry list of accusations. From what I could gather, Lydia and Clark were some kind of item during her senior year of high school and extending into her freshman year at Berkeley. Clark snagged a baseball scholarship at USC, so after a torrid summer they embarked on a long-distance affair. The letter—and the benefit of hindsight—suggested it was doomed from the start.

Clark had taken the train to Berkeley for a weekend visit. He and Lydia went to a party. For some reason, Lydia pitched a nutty and left the party after only a couple of hours and eight or twelve Jägermeister hits. Clark, whose inhibitions and scruples—at least those he had at the ripe age of eighteen—were also substantially impaired, was later discovered skin-surfing with a coed in the spare bedroom. Word got back to Lydia after Clark returned to Los Angeles, resulting in the letter. Lydia alternately excoriated Clark for going behind her back, even as she seemed angry that, if he really wanted to be with other women, he hadn't asked her to join in.

I suppose that should have been provocative, but I live in San Francisco, so…That was it. The letter ended with Lydia demanding that Clark apologize, or things were over for them. It was signed plainly with her first name only, dashed out furiously and with several heavy-handed lines drawn underneath for emphasis.

I wondered why it was never put in the mail. Did Clark call Lydia just as she finished penning it, and was all resolved in happy tears to the backdrop of a flourish of imaginary violins? Perhaps Lydia decided a two-timing creep like Clark wasn't even worth the price of a stamp and stashed the letter in a drawer somewhere. Did fate in the form of a hot new infatuation on campus intercede, providing Lydia the opportunity to give Clark the old heave-ho? Or did Clark break things off after sampling and liking some free range strange?

Questions like this keep me awake at night.

I plugged Clark Riesenberger's address into my GPS and did a drive-by. Progress is a cruel taskmaster. The address on Lydia's envelope was now a strip mall containing a bodega, an insurance company, a charismatic storefront church, a bail bondsman, a tax preparer, and a weed dispensary. Didn't feel like wasting the trip, so I popped in on the bail bondsman and handed him my card. Never know when you might need to scare up some pocket change chasing skips. Hit the dispensary and bought an eighth of Durban Poison for Heidi. I'm more a beer and wine kind of guy, but she's artsy-fartsy and enjoys a toke now and then.

Back at my Russian Hill house, I opened up CyberShamus and did a search for Clark Riesenberger, USC graduate. Apparently, he was still alive, but I couldn't locate an address anywhere. It happens sometimes, even in an increasingly unprivate society. Some people go all Luddite and find a way to separate themselves entirely from the grid. Folks who live in cars don't hang out mailboxes. Same for those who convert school buses into rolling meth labs with cots in the back. Homeless people aren't on a lot of lists. I wondered whether Clark Riesenberger had fallen on the hardest of times. Didn't mean I couldn't locate him if I needed to, but the looking would be a bitch.

TWENTY

I arrived at the Top of the Mark, the rooftop bar at the Mark Hopkins Hotel, dressed to kill. I was meeting the estranged wife of a city supervisor. I didn't want to disappoint the paparazzi.

Maisie Blah Blah Blah Blah Pauch arrived before me. She recognized me by my cane and the devil-may-care panache that followed me around like a process server. She was shorter than I expected, probably a little over five feet tall in bare feet, flatteringly curvaceous, and had the kind of blonde hair you can't buy in a box at the drugstore. It fell around her face in a complimentary pageboy cut. She wore a shimmery dress and dangerously precarious stiletto heels. If I had come dressed to kill, she was loaded for bear.

We took a table next to a floor-to-ceiling window facing the Transamerica Tower and the bay. The sun setting on the far side of the Golden Gate cast long shadows across the city as commuters made their way to the suburbs after a long day in the salt mines. We plowed through the basic introductions, and I ordered a Manhattan. She already had a glass of sauvignon blanc.

"Got some ID, Sport?" she said. "I have to be careful, you know. I might be divorcing my piece of shit cheating husband, but we are still married, and I need to know you aren't some sort of opportunistic reporter."

I handed her my card and showed her the copy of my PI license in my wallet. She stared at both for a while, her face mildly twisted in frustration.

"Fuck this shit." She fished around in her clutch purse for a pair of cheater glasses. "Thought I'd bull my way through, but fact is I can't see bloody fuck up close without these."

She slipped the glasses on and looked at the card again.

"*Eamon Gold, Discreet Investigations*," she read out loud. "Did I pronounce that right? Eamon?"

"Eamon it is," I said.

"What kind of name is that?"

"Irish, by way of Wales. My mother's side of the family."

"What did you do to your leg?"

"Some dude in a bar was mouthing off. Said short women weren't worth the trouble. I was compelled to set him straight."

"Looks like you failed."

"Appearances deceive. I walked out. He didn't."

"You're lying," she said.

"I am. Was it impressive?"

"You could use some practice. That's a compliment. You wanted to know about Lydia Carlisle."

"Yes."

"Blast from the past. Haven't heard her name in years. Haven't thought about her. What's she up to these days?"

"That," I said, "is the question of the hour. She disappeared a long time ago. I'm trying to find her."

"Why?"

"She ran off with a man who stole a great deal of money."

"So you're looking for the money."

"So young, yet so cynical," I said, as the waitress returned with my drink. I took a sip. It was excellent, but as a long-time supporter of the Top of the Mark I expected no less.

"Not so young," she said, angling for a compliment.

"Three out of four husbands disagree."

She smiled and sipped from her wine glass. "You're a charmer. Not hard to look at, either. Interested in shooting for Number Five?"

"I'm in a thing," I said. "Sort of."

"It's the *sort of* that makes the difference. Doesn't matter. You're attractive, in a dangerous, hunky, ex-athlete kind of way."

"I hear I always look better in subdued lighting," I said. "In pitch dark, I'm adorable."

"I'll be the judge of that. Sadly, I've become accustomed to a particular lifestyle, and I don't think a private cop can afford it."

"Don't be so certain. The job I'm on could yield a payday of a couple million dollars."

"Yeah…" she said, her voice trailing off. "Close, but no cigar. That kind of money gets you in the game, but nowhere near the chapel door. What do you want to know about Lydia?"

"Anything you have. I hoped she might have tried to contact you at some point. Social media, that sort of thing."

"Politicians' wives aren't allowed much of an online presence, unless it's mediated by some flunky. Too much chance of saying something embarrassing. I have a couple of accounts, but I don't write the posts, and I never check the messages. If she had tried to get in touch, I'd never have seen it. Beyond that, all I have of her are memories."

"Care to share some of them?"

"Depends," she said. "I have all night. Why don't you take me to dinner and expense it to your client?"

Maisie's connection to the Board of Supervisors snagged us a table at the Nob Hill Club in the Mark Hopkins, an intimate, wooden wainscoted lounge where the vegetarian offerings topped the average worker's daily salary, and a dish with protein could put your bank account in a coma. What the hell. It was all on Jackson Pike's nickel anyway, so I ordered the Angus ribeye. Maisie ordered the sea bass, protesting all the time that she had to look after her figure if she was to harpoon another power husband.

We shared the green garbanzo hummus and split a bottle of Corona Farms pinot noir as we talked.

"Lydia was a wild child from the get-go," she said, as she dipped a crisp pita chip in the hummus. "Probably what attracted me to her. I was sort of shy, easily influenced by more socially adept kids."

"You appear to have recovered nicely," I said.

"Yeah, once these came in." She pointed at her chest. "All of a sudden, I was the center of attention, and I learned to adapt. But that was later. When Lydia and I were buddies, she was the leader and I was the follower. And boy did she lead."

"How do you mean?"

"She was always precocious. The first to smoke. First to smoke a joint. The first to go out on a date. The first to go all the way. Like she was in a huge rush to grow up. Back in the day, we'd call her *fast and easy*. Funny. These days, she'd be just one of the crowd. Kids these days are humping like bunnies almost before they have pubes. Not back then. Lydia blazed the trail, and I sort of followed along. She was my first woman, you know."

"Beg pardon?"

"My first girl-on-girl fling. I suppose, today, it's sort of quaint and cute, but back then nobody talked much about it."

"The love which dare not speak its name," I observed.

"Well, it may have whispered it a little. I went over to Lydia's house. Her parents were out, so naturally we raided their liquor cabinet. Lydia had a couple of joints squirreled away in her bedroom. We were—what?—maybe fifteen at the time. I had a crush on a boy in my biology class, but of course I hadn't done anything about it except complain to Lydia that he never paid attention to me. She asked what I'd do if he did. I was clueless. Didn't know jack shit about boys. Had never seen a dick angry in my life, except in some *Playgirl* magazines Lydia kept under her mattress. Lydia asked if I knew how to kiss a boy. When I said I didn't, she offered to teach me. She taught me, all right. Taught me plenty. We fooled around off and on for the next year, and by then I was getting a lot of looks from the boys, including my Bio buddy. Turns out he was my first guy. Go figure. I've had a few other women over the years, when I got tired of body hair and egos and masculine swagger, but it was all for shits and giggles. Nothing serious. My closet might have a revolving door, but I spend ninety-nine percent of my time on the straight side. Am I embarrassing you?"

"Not at all," I said, looking at the Corona Farms wine bottle and thinking of one of my former clients, a gay winery exec named Asa Corona, who had bottled it. "This is San Francisco, right? Comes with the territory. Different strokes for different folks."

"Sweetie, I do believe you just quoted the California state motto."

"When did you last see Lydia?"

We were interrupted by the waiter, who arrived with our dishes. I took the opportunity to refresh Maisie's glass.

"Must have been..." she stopped and contemplated the time. "Wow. Somewhere between twenty-five and thirty years ago. Let's see. I guess it was a high school graduation trip. A bunch of us went to Tahoe for a few days, to blow off steam and live it up before summer jobs kicked in. I drove, and Lydia rode with me and a couple of classmates. I think that was the last time we slept together too. I started work the next week at Great America amusement park, and at the end of the summer I headed to college back east. By the time I returned home to stay, she was gone."

"Did she ever mention a man named Eddie Rice?"

"Hell, Lydia talked about lots of guys. There was a new one every week. She probably had to have her cooch re-sleeved by the time she was thirty, if she made it that far."

"Why do you say that?"

"Lydia was born to die young. She took risks. Always upping the ante. Maybe she was easily bored and needed the stimulation. Maybe she was mentally ill and had to have the complete attention of others to feel like she existed. The last

103

time I saw her, she had already ditched weed for blow, which was everywhere at the time. Ever been to the Cliff House?"

The Cliff House was just that, a resort mounted on a cliff overlooking the Golden Gate, with sheer drops to the beach below.

"Sure," I said.

"We went there our senior year. Some kind of school function. I caught Lydia sitting on the fucking edge of the cliff, dangling her feet over a hundred-foot drop. One slip, and she'd be dead. I asked her to back away, afraid she'd fall. She cartwheeled along the edge. Scared the piss out of me. That's how she was. Always putting her skin on the line. Someday, her luck was bound to run out, right? Not to change the subject, but how did you know to look for me?"

"I've been hired by Lydia's stepfather to find her. He rummaged through some of her personal items and found a lot of notes Lydia and you passed back and forth in school."

"Really? I'd love to see those. Should be a hoot. You know who you should talk to? Sonny Malehala."

"Hawaiian?"

"Beats the shit out of me. He's some kind of Polynesian, but from where exactly I couldn't say. He was a halfback on our high school football team. Sweet boy, face like that bald action movie guy who used to be a wrestler. Muscles on top of his muscles. Nice dancer."

"Is he still around?"

"Damned if I know. Haven't seen him in almost as long as I haven't seen Lydia. She and I both did him, at different times, during senior year. Anyway, he and Lydia were tight the last time I saw her. Maybe he kept in touch."

"How about a boy named Clark Riesenberger?"

She nearly spit wine on the tablecloth.

"Clark! Where'd you dig him up?"

"In Lydia's effects was a letter she wrote to Riesenberger but never mailed. Sounded like she was breaking things off."

"Lydia wrote a letter? Hard to imagine. That is *so* not her style."

"How do you mean?" I asked.

"She needs human contact. Dotes on it. Craves it like an addict. Not like her to write everything down and send it, when she could groove on the drama of a face-to-face confrontation, preferably over scorched earth. She was kind of like that. Clark Riesenberger, huh? Yeah, I know him. Randy Bullcock."

"Say again?" I said.

"Name he goes by now, at least in the business."

"Business."

She sipped at her wine and gazed at me over the top of her glass. Her eyes were shiny. She slid the glass back onto the cloth and leaned forward.

"Clark Riesenberger had the biggest cock I ever saw," she said, in a dramatic whisper. She leaned back. "Probably the biggest *you* ever saw. I mean, we're talking Guinness Book of World Records here. I think his mother was frightened by a Louisville Slugger when she was pregnant. Which is kind of appropriate, since he went to college on a baseball scholarship. He could knock one out of the park with that boner."

"He is amply endowed," I summarized.

"And how. He's almost a freak of nature, poor guy. We were at a party, senior year of high school. Clark had eyed Lydia since the first of the school year, but they never really connected until spring. Both were drinking, and Clark took Lydia's hand and led her down the hall to one of the bedrooms. Next thing, we hear Lydia screaming, *'Not on your life!'* We thought maybe he was strangling her or something. I threw open the door, and there it was. You ever see the Coit Tower when it's all lit up at night? It was a lot like that. Like, to scale."

"I see."

"Couldn't miss it. Kinda dominated the landscape. Turns out all the screaming was Lydia being Lydia. Dramatic, you know? Nothing intimidated that bitch. She had every intention of climbing that mountain. I did him later, when I was on a holiday trip home from college. Son of a bitch bruised me all to hell and gave me a UTI."

"What became of him?"

"The baseball thing didn't work out. He shot for the majors with Double A talent. He bounced around some stanky-ass podunk bus-and-truck minor league teams in the Midwest for six or seven seasons, playing dimly lit dustbowls ringed by cornfields for two or three hundred hayseeds, but that's as far as he got. He futzed around for a few years, doing this and that, until he met some chick in a bar who had connections in the porn biz. She…um…auditioned him in a one-night stand, and the rest is the stuff of legend. I ran into him at a high school reunion a few years back, before I met Pauch. We got totally blazed and hooked up again for old time's sake. I didn't walk right for a week. He told me he was doing skin flicks for some outfit in town under the name Randy Bullcock. I have a couple of his DVDs at home. Want to come over for Movie Night sometime? You can bring your sort-of thing."

"You have any way to contact him?"

"Not a clue. He told me he was under contract to a specific studio, though."

"Didn't say which one?"

"It was a nostalgic booty call fueled by booze and skunkweed. We weren't exchanging business cards, Gold. Tell you the truth, once every ten years with Clark is plenty. I know a lot of women are total size queens, but a guy can be *too* big, know what I mean?"

"I'll take your word for it," I said.

TWENTY-ONE

I probably could have downloaded a ream of information on Randy Bullcock in a couple of minutes, but sometimes you just want to do things the old-fashioned way, slapping shoe leather on sidewalk concrete.

It seems quaint—even a little archaic—in the age of endless free online porn, but a few brick and mortar adult video stores yet linger in the erotic entertainment wilderness. To survive, many of them have diversified into intimate apparel and marital aids, but there's still the core business of peddling skin flicks. Puck's 24-Hour DVD was just such an enterprise, and it had the added benefit of being run by a former client, a guy named Robin Ruffalo. Rob was squat, bald, round, hairy, and in every other conceivable way as trollish a human as you are likely to encounter. I'm not being cruel. In the land of genetic jackpots, Rob had drawn a handful of defective scratch-offs, but he also possessed something of an off-putting personality. His hygiene could bear some attention as well.

Rob sat on a stool behind the counter when I walked into Puck's, past display cases filled with silicone phalluses of every hue and shape, cupless bras and crotchless panties, vibrators (both AC and DC), leather accessories, and something called a 'backdoor intruder', which I suspected had nothing to do with breaching locked houses. All the stuff in the case was dusty.

"Whatcha got, Gold?" Rob growled as he slid off the stool and dropped half a foot to the ground. "I know you ain't here as a payin' customer. Whad'ja do to your leg?"

"There's a potentially fatal error on page one-hundred-three of *The Joy of Sex,*" I said. "Someday, you are going to have to tell me how you stay in business. I never see any customers here."

"We do a lot of mail-order," he said. "Help you?"

I had long harbored suspicions that Puck's 24-Hour DVD laundered money for the mob. It would have been impolite to mention that to Rob, though, especially when I needed a favor.

"Looking for a video with some guy named Randy Bullcock," I said.

"Fuckin' freak show," Rob said.

"You refer, I presume, to his...ah, anatomical curiosity?"

"Guy's packin' a fuckin' fire hose. Got fuckin' elephantitis of the schwantz. Know what they call him in the business?"

"What?"

"The Log Splitter."

"Ouch," I said.

"Follow me." Rob waddled down an aisle until he reached a rack filled with cellophane shrink-wrapped DVDs. He grabbed one off the rack and handed it to me. The cover was a fleshy montage of tangled bodies, gynecological closeups, and in the center a peroxide blond woman apparently strangling on what appeared to be a pink, veiny oil pipeline.

"Randy Bullcock," Rob said, as if introducing nobility at a royal ball. He swept his arm in the air, as if embracing the entire rack. "It's all Randy Bullcock. Guy's a fuckin' franchise." He handed me the video. I read the credits on the back and saw a familiar name.

"How much?" I asked.

"You want to *buy* this?" Rob said.

"You could give it to me."

Rob snatched the carton from me and peered through his bifocals at the back. "Sure, I'll give it to you. Label says I'll give it to you for twenty-nine-ninety-five and tax. What you want this for, anyway?"

I smiled as I pulled out my wallet. "Present for a friend."

———

That night, Heidi and I cooked out at the Montara House. I grilled inch-thick bone-in pork chops and silver queen corn, and served it with pinto beans and onions, balsamic mustard greens, sweet Jiffy Mix corn muffins, and tonkatsu sauce. Sated, we retired to the sofa, opened a second bottle of Corona Farms red, and I put on the Randy Bullcock video I'd purchased at Puck's.

"This is new," Heidi said, as the credits began to roll. "But not unwelcome. I was getting tired of all the superhero movies...Holy *shit*."

Randy Bullcock made his first appearance.

"This isn't CGI?" she asked. "Or some kind of prosthesis, like that kid used in **Boogie Nights?**"

"I am assured by a satisfied consumer that what you are seeing is one-hundred percent legit." I said.

"Holy *shit!*" she said again.

"They call him The Log Splitter."

"You bought this for me?"

"Something to keep you company when I'm away."

"This has something to do with your case?"

"Yes," I said. "Hard to take your eyes away, isn't it? Have you ever seen anything like that?"

"Sure. Just not on a human. Can he pick up peanuts with it?"

"Want to meet him?" I handed her the DVD case and pointed to the fine print at the bottom of the box. *SWSX Productions, Marin County, California.*

"Simon?" she asked.

"A happy coincidence. Randy Bullcock, whose real name is Clark Riesenberger, works for the only pornographer I know personally. Called him this afternoon. He's shooting tomorrow. Said he'd get me some face time with this guy."

"He has a face?"

"Want to tag along?" I asked.

"Hell, yeah," she said. "The Grand Canyon. The Great Wall. The Eiffel Tower. Some things you just have to see in person."

TWENTY-TWO

The air was warm for October, with a slight tinge of leaf smoke, as Heidi and I crossed the Golden Gate into Marin County. The sky spanned over us like a transparent blue globe, not a cloud in sight.

We were in Heidi's Miata, because my leg still ached when I took the wheel. She sat in the driver seat, her hair pulled back in a blonde French braid and covered with a silk Hermes scarf. I had dressed down for the occasion, jeans and a long-sleeved blue oxford cloth shirt, with a light houndstooth tweed jacket.

Heidi leaned her head back against the headrest and smiled as she kneaded my good thigh. It was okay. She was permitted to do that.

Our destination was an estate in the land of Luke Skywalker and towering redwoods, belonging to a former client and longtime drinking buddy Simon Wood. Simon was a pornographer, one of the classy ones who produce and direct high-budget feature films with only the hottest stars and honest-to-gosh scripts. The library in Simon's house features a glass-front bookcase containing no fewer than thirty-one AVN Award statuettes—Oscar-like figures depicting an intertwined naked couple—for directing and producing. Simon was one of the last adult directors to abandon film for digital media, and it still sat in his craw like a live sea urchin.

I'd introduced Heidi to Simon a year or so earlier, when I was tracking down an illegal Chinese immigrant woman named Wei Ma Lo. It turned out she had found highly lucrative employment in the fuck film industry, working under the name Sugar Wei, and she was one of Simon's hottest stars. Sugar had left the business to work for attorney Louis Gai, the grass sandal of the Sung Chow Li tong in Chinatown. Knowing Louis as I do, I was uncertain whether her new employment constituted a zig toward grace or a zag deeper into the maw of iniquity.

Heidi flicked the wheel right and left as she navigated Simon's long, winding drive up the side of Mount Tamalpais, and we heaved through a canopy of trees into a circular driveway only slightly smaller than the Place de la Concorde in Paris.

Simon's front door was ostentatious and intimidating— twin monoliths of hand carved Spanish cypress over fifteen feet tall, embellished with masterfully wrought tendrils, vines, and leaves. I rang the bell. The doors swung open automatically, admitting us to an open courtyard entranceway, beyond which stood a second set of glass doors which I knew could stop a fifty-caliber slug. They slid open, and Simon strode through, his arms wide.

He was a tall man, an inch or two over six feet, and built like an NFL halfback—wide, muscular, and yet somehow limber and quick. His head was shaved completely bald, and one blue eye pointed off slightly to the outside, just enough to make him seem swaggering without being overtly threatening. His teeth were polar white, and straight as a picket fence. He wore a form-fitting pullover sport shirt, and cargo shorts that revealed legs Schwarzenegger would envy. Since I had seen him last, he had grown a thick mustache mottled with gray. He smelled of spicy cologne, judiciously applied.

"Eamon! Heidi!" He squealed as he wrapped his arms around both of us and gave us both a kiss on the cheek. Did I mention Simon is the irrepressible type? "Haven't seen you two since that Sugar Wei business a couple of years ago. Sure I can't convince you to take a turn in front of the cameras, Heidi? You'd be sensational!"

The first time I introduced Heidi to Simon, he thought I was bringing him talent. He immediately grabbed her breasts to see if they were real. I had to give Heidi credit. She handled it like a trooper.

"It's still a *no*," she said. "At least the sex part. Naked extra? Maybe."

"It wouldn't be fair to the audience," he said. "We'll just keep this a friendly relationship."

He turned to me.

"So you want to meet Randy Bullcock?"

"I want to meet Clark Riesenberger," I said. "I'm sure Randy has a lot of interesting stories, but the ones I want to hear are about the time before he became a famous stunt dick."

"Please, Eamon! Randy is *so* much more than that. Do you know, he studied under Uta Hagen in New York? The boy is an *ac*-tor. The real McCoy."

"No offense, Simon," I said, "but if he's such a great actor, why isn't he working down in Hollywood?"

"It is *such* a cruel business. You'll see when you meet him. It's *so* sad. Come on inside, you two. You know where everything is. Randy's out back, by the pool. We aren't shooting for another several hours, so he's just working on his tan."

"All over, I presume?" Heidi said.

"*Mais oui!*" Simon said. "Our audience expects nothing less. Tan lines are *soooo* 1970s."

On a closed-circuit screen next to the front door, a car pulled into the circular parking lot. Simon saw it as well.

"My camera crew just arrived. Need to help them unload. Make yourself at home. Craft table is in the kitchen. Have a beer or some wine. Kick back. Enjoy yourselves." He pinched my cheek. It felt like he burst a blood vessel. Then he hustled toward the towering cypress doors to greet his crew. Heidi and I found the kitchen quickly. I grabbed a bottle of Anchor Steam, and Heidi had a sauvignon blanc. We had eaten brunch before leaving the city, so we left the craft table unmolested, at least for the moment.

We stepped out onto the lanai which opened onto the swimming pool. Heidi pointed toward a pair of chaises on the other side, only one of which was occupied.

"Randy Bullcock," she whispered.

"Down, girl."

We circled the pool. Clark Riesenberg, as a high school classmate of Lydia Carlisle and Maisie Duncan, had to be pushing fifty. Randy Bullcock showed no indication of being near that age. The man looked as if he could be in his middle thirties. He sat on the chaise on top of the robe he had doffed to take full advantage of the midday sun. The tropical aroma of sunscreen wafted around him. His flat washboard stomach and carefully sculpted muscles suggested a much younger man, or countless gym hours. The feature attraction flopped between his legs on the chaise, looking somewhat as if it might coil and strike at any moment. He wore sunglasses, but he took them off as we approached.

I understood immediately what Simon meant about the cruelty of Hollywood. The camera didn't capture it as adeptly as the human eye. In person, Randy Bullcock was the spitting image of a perennial box office cash cow known widely for his action films and his offbeat religion. Casting directors probably took one look at him and said, "We already have one of those," and that was that. Clark Riesenberger didn't have a prayer in mainstream films, where he would always be compared to his much more successful doppelganger, but Randy Bullcock's uncanny resemblance made him a natural for porn parodies of popular movies, such as *Emission Probable*, *Lays of Thunder*, *Thighs Wide Open*, and his seminal masterpiece *A Few Dozen Good Men*, the marketing catchphrase of which was "You Can't Handle the Bull!"

"You're the detective Simon told me about?" he asked.

I handed him my card. Heidi hovered beside me, taking in the scenery.

"Private cop," I said. I introduced him to Heidi, who struggled to make eye contact.

"Please, take a seat," he said. "And, if you don't mind, call me Clark. I'm only Randy on camera."

"But you're always slinging *that*, right?" Heidi asked.

Clark laughed. He had a pleasant laugh. He didn't seem to carry the hard edge I'd noted in some porn actors.

"It's not a Snap-On. I'll cover up if you like," he said. "Twenty years in the business, I could probably walk down

Pacific Street like this and never crack a blush. If it makes you uncomfortable, though..." he reached for his towel.

"Please, don't," Heidi said. "Not on my account. You're fine."

"Thanks," he said, casting the towel to one side. "I appreciate it. We're shooting underwater this afternoon. Skin tones wash out in the pool. Want to work on my tan a little beforehand."

"Underwater?" Heidi asked.

"A fetish thing. There's a whole niche market who love to see people get it on underwater. I love doing the scenes, too. Not as hot as working under the lights, and the pay is higher."

"Why's that?" I said.

"Takes twice as long to shoot. This ain't a snorkel. If you watch the finished scene, you'll notice the camera changes position every twenty seconds or so. So, we shoot twenty seconds underwater, and then we breathe and shoot another twenty seconds."

"You keep going down and coming up for air, then," Heidi said.

Clark smiled at her. She smiled back. I considered updating my Tinder account.

"About that," I said. "The 'twenty years in the business' thing, not the...you know. Underwater thing. By my calculations, you're pushing fifty."

"And how do I keep getting adult film work as a codger?" he said. "Easy. There's a market for middle-aged actors. Boomers, man. They dug in and aren't letting go. The Sixties kids are retiring, with lots of disposable income and a burning desire not to relinquish their youth and sexuality. If anything, they become even more sexually adventurous as they age. Half the swing clubs in San Francisco cater to people over fifty. It's like a sea of gray. Granny porn is a real thing these days. People want to watch other people who look like them. I may not be attractive to the Millennials, unless they have serious daddy issues, but for the Beatles' babies, guys my age in the business are kings of the hill. That's a good thing, because I can't see a point in the future where I'm not working. Porn doesn't exactly have a great pension system. So, what can I do for you?"

"I'm looking for Lydia Carlisle," I said.

He cocked his head at the name. "Wow. Haven't heard about her in ages. Looking for her? Is she missing?"

"For over a quarter century."

"No shit. Really?"

"I take it you haven't been in touch."

"No. Not since...well, I guess it was college. She was at Berkeley. I was at UCLA."

"Baseball scholarship," I said. His eyes narrowed.

"You know things," he said.

"I interviewed Maisie Duncan the other night. She told me about your career."

"Maisie? How is she?"

"Scouting around for Hubby Number Five. If you have twenty million or so lying around, you might get into the running."

"Maisie is wound way too tight for me. One thing about making your living the way I do, there's lots of downtime to kick back and contemplate the important things in life. Maisie's head spends too much time in next month or next year. I'm content with today, right now. So things didn't work out with the Supervisor, huh? Maybe I'll give her a call anyway. Grab a drink. Did Maisie place me with Lydia Carlisle?"

"Lydia's stepfather gave me a box of letters and other notes. She wrote you a letter but never mailed it."

"You read it?"

"I'm not psychic."

"What did it say?"

I pulled it from my jacket pocket and handed it to him. He opened it and scanned the first couple of paragraphs.

"Wow," he said, looking up. "She was pissed."

"Long distance relationships," I said. "What're you gonna do?"

"*When I'm not near the girl I love, I love the girl I'm near*," Clark sang, with impressive pitch. "We were kids. Eighteen. Nineteen. What did we know? It would be quaint if it weren't so sad."

"Sad?"

"I suppose I knew quickly how...*different* Lydia was. Her head didn't work like most people's. She was overly dramatic, had mood swings that came on like thunderstorms, and an antipathy toward her father that was kind of scary."

"Antipathy?" I said.

"What? I pork people for a living, so I can't be erudite?" He chuckled. "Relax, Mr. Gold. I'm used to it. I may have been on a sports scholarship, but I took my education seriously. Majored in psychology."

"Why didn't you become a psychologist? It's easy in this state."

"I thought baseball would pay better. Best laid plans. I don't think I ever made more than twenty thousand and change in a single season. And then I was out on my can. I could have gone back to grad school if I wanted. No problem. I just met Nadezhda first."

"Nadezhda?"

"Nadezhda Von Squirt. Professional name. She introduced me to Simon, and the rest is history."

"Porn pays better than baseball?"

"Porn pays better than most things."

"How?" Heidi asked.

"I don't understand," he said.

"Where does the money come from?" she said. "You can access skin flicks anywhere on the Internet for free. Who pays for this stuff?"

He laughed. "Next time you wander by a porn site, count the advertisements. Sex is just the draw. The ads are the product. Every major porn website in the country is controlled by a single company. Every. Single. One. That company pays well for quality programming, because the advertisements on the sites make them very, very rich. Also, the websites have both free and paid sections. My films all run in the paid sections, so if you want to watch ol' Randy Bullcock in action, you have to pony up. I get a cut—a very small cut percentage-wise—of those subscriptions, but I work in volume, so it adds up. There are still brick and mortar video stores, and online sales count for a lot. Thank goodness I don't have to worry about any of that. I just show up, let Tantor here do its thing, and my agent sends me a fat check. The rest of my life belongs to me. I won't tell you how much I made last year, but I have a house overlooking the beach in Malibu, and if I decide to make a run at Maisie, my portfolio would probably take me to the head of the line. But, tell me. How did Lydia disappear?"

I told him about the armored car robbery and Eddie Rice. I asked him whether he had ever heard of Rice.

"Nope. Doesn't ring a bell."

"You said Lydia had a lot of antipathy for her father. What did you mean?"

Clark sighed and looked past us, where Simon was showing the camera crew the angles he wanted to shoot that afternoon.

"It wasn't just the armored car robbery," he said. "Demons lived inside Lydia's head. Their favorite hobby was squirting lighter fluid on her soul and striking matches. Anything I tell you about Lydia has only about a fifty percent chance of being true, because the line between truth and lies in her head shifted with the tides. So, what I'm about to tell you might be true. It might not."

"What's that?" I asked.

"Look, Mr. Gold, Lydia and I were a hot item in high school. That was over thirty years ago. I went to L.A., she went to Berkeley. I was still a teenager, just a hormone in sneakers. One thing about being hung. Word gets around. Every coed on campus wanted a peek. I tried to remain faithful, but I was a kid. That shit lasted about a month and a half, and then it was game on. I got cocky and made it with one of her friends at a party in Berkeley. That's when she wrote this letter. We broke up before the end of my first semester, and to tell you the truth, I haven't seen her since then."

"I get it. Time might have altered some of your memories. I'm not a prosecuting attorney. I'm only looking for trends. The details may not be important. So what is it that might or might not be true?"

"Graduation night in high school. There was a huge party at some rich student's house. Lydia and I were hot on it at the time, going at it like crazy monkeys on meth. Sex was new and I wanted to do it every fucking day, twice on Sunday. Lydia and I got loaded, smoked a little weed, and went looking for a quiet empty room. We locked the door and started throwing down, and then she just...stopped and stared off into space. She didn't say a word. Was barely breathing. Then, she shook her head a couple of times, and looked at me as if I was someone completely different. *'Daddy?'* she said, in this little girl voice. *'I didn't mean to be bad.'* She stood up, walked into the corner where we'd tossed our clothes, and pulled my belt through the loops in my pants. She walked back over to me, almost like she was sleepwalking, and she handed me the belt and bent over the side of the bed, like she was presenting her ass for a whipping."

"Holy shit," Heidi said, softly.

"Exactly what I said," Clark continued. "Maybe you've already heard Lydia was dramatic. You never knew when she was actually hurting and when she was faking it for attention. I tossed the belt aside and turned her over. She arched her back and made a grunting sound, and then stared off into space again. A minute later, she was the usual Lydia, but a little confused. I told her what she'd done, and she started crying. Then she told me some shit I've never been able to wipe from my memory. Best thing that ever happened to Lydia was when her dad was sent off to prison. Probably the worst thing, too, because she never had the opportunity to confront him over what he did to her."

"How do you mean?" I asked.

"Let's just say the father-daughter dynamic between Lydia and her dad crossed some serious boundaries. The way she put it, he hadn't made an honest dollar in years. He was away for days at a time, and when he was home his parenting skills betrayed his lack of practice or even interest. When Lydia misbehaved, she got the belt. When Daddy felt bad about whipping her, later, he tried to make up. In this case, making up didn't involve a trip to the ice cream parlor."

"I'm beginning to understand why he was so angry she ran off with Eddie Rice," I said.

Clark said. "I'm no shrink, though I've played one once or twice in the flicks." He winked at Heidi. "Last psych class I took was over twenty-five years ago, so what do I know? But I recall one lecturer in Abnormal, who talked about personality disorders. She alleged that every woman she ever diagnosed with borderline personality disorder had been sexually abused. I don't know if it's true or not, but if—and that's a huge *if*—what Lydia told me about her dad was for real, it explained a lot of her behavior."

"Borderline personality disorder," I repeated.

"And we have reached the extent of my clinical expertise," he said, smiling. "Not that I ever had any. A real shrink could explain it a lot better than I can."

"Fortunately," I said. "I know one."

TWENTY-THREE

I was quiet on the drive back to San Francisco, slumped in the passenger seat of Heidi's Miata, lost in thought.

"What do you think?" Heidi asked, halfway across the bridge.

"It's fascinating," I said. "But not helpful. I'm learning a lot about Lydia, but none of it pulls me any closer to finding out where she went, and what became of Eddie Rice."

"And the money."

"Most importantly the money."

"But you'll figure it out."

"Pull enough threads…"

"And the sweater ravels. So which string do you pull next?"

"I want to know more about this borderline personality disorder thing. I have another couple of friends of Lydia's to interview. No rush. It's been thirty years. Waiting another day won't hurt."

———————

Sonny Malehala might have been a hot-shit high school football star, but his life since had taken a decidedly different turn.

While he was pushing fifty, he had weathered the years well. He had the sort of shape you earn through thousands of reps on each machine at the gym. I could tell he had been handsome enough in his youth, but as he approached fifty his face was angular and shadowed, and a little foreboding. He had shaved his head completely bald. Someone along the line had broken his nose, and it hadn't set properly. Standing over six feet tall and weighing roughly the same as a school bus, he was intimidating enough without the obvious bulge in his jacket made by the automatic pistol wedged under his arm in a shoulder rig. I considered showing him mine for comparison, but I wasn't wearing it. Something in his eyes made me wish I was.

My discreet inquiries into his history, before I contacted him to meet, had informed me he was muscle for Junius 'JuneBug' Bugliosi, the aging chief of the dwindling remnants of San Francisco's Sicilian mob. Their influence had been reduced markedly over the years by the influx of the Chinatown triads and MS-13 gangs traveling up the state after entering from Guatemala, but JuneBug still had the juice to make you disappear if adequately riled. I had a feeling Sonny Malehala had dumped more than one body for JuneBug over the years.

I had my own reasons to regard JuneBug with caution. A year earlier, I'd helped Daron Corona bury four members of the Bugliosi gang in an unmarked trench under a new stand of muscadine grapes in the Corona Farms vineyard. I was confident they acted without JuneBug's knowledge when he attacked the vineyard, but I couldn't be absolutely certain. Since then, I'd given JuneBug a wide berth.

We sat in a Swenson's on Hyde Street. It was the most innocuous place I could think of to meet a known gangster. Everyone loves ice cream, and I figured a nonthreatening venue would get us off to the right start. He gestured across the booth to my cane. "What did you do to your leg?"

"Shark attack," I said. "Next time I'll take a bigger boat."

He chuckled and sipped at his coffee.

"Cards on the table," I told Malehala. "I know you work for Mr. Bugliosi."

"I have no idea what you're talking about," he said. His voice was wheezy, as if he'd just run the four-forty in dress shoes.

"Sure. And that hand-cannon under your arm is for personal protection. For the record, I don't give a damn, and the reason I wanted to meet has nothing to do with JuneBug..."

Malehala immediately bristled, and his face flushed. He raised a single eyebrow, in an expression that told me I'd stepped over a line. I'd forgotten that Bugliosi wasn't fond of his nickname.

"...Mr. Bugliosi," I corrected. "I'm here to discuss Lydia Carlisle."

His entire demeanor flipped in an instant. Briefly, I thought I saw a dribble of compassion in his obsidian eyes. "You've seen Lydia?"

"No. I'm looking for her. One of her friends referred you to me."

"Maisie," he said, quietly. "Has to be. She's the only connection between me and Lydia. How is Maisie?"

"On the rebound, apparently. She's ditching Husband Number Four and casting about for a replacement."

"I might give her a call," he said. "For old time's sake. Why are you looking for Lydia?"

"Her stepfather hired me. You know she's been missing for a quarter century?"

"Sure. Haven't thought about Lydia in a while, of course. Or Maisie, for that matter. That all seems like a long time ago."

"She apparently ran off with a man named Eddie Rice."

He shook his head. "Doesn't mean anything to me. Never heard the name. Was he in school with us?"

"He was considerably older."

"I'm not surprised. Lydia preferred older men. Daddy issues."

"You seem well-read."

"What? I wear a gun and work for a mobster, so I must be some sort of ignorant goon?"

"No offense intended," I said.

He clamped one meaty paw over my hand and pressed down, scowling. It felt like a semi had parked on it. "You think I'm funny? So I'm some kind of clown? I amuse you?" He grinned and released my hand. "I'm fuckin' with you, Gold. Relax. Got the whole scene memorized. Yeah, I picked up some college back in the day. Played rugby on a scholarship."

"Not football?"

"Football's for pussies. Rugby players leave meat on the field and eat their dead. Anyway, for the record, you aren't dealing with some deadhead gorilla. What do you want to know about Lydia?"

"You already answered one question. Eddie Rice."

"Like I said. Never heard of him."

"How about Lydia? When was the last time you saw her?"

"A year or so after high school graduation. A long time ago."

"How'd you get hooked up with the Bugliosi organization?"

"I thought we were here to talk about Lydia."

"I'm curious."

"You want to be careful about that, Gold. Mr. Bugliosi cherishes his privacy. He doesn't take kindly to people poking their noses into his business."

"And I have no interest in his business, so that works out. I'm curious about you."

"Why?"

"It's my nature."

"You know, I heard about you," he said. "Rumor has it you played a role in starting the war in Chinatown a few years back. You still working for Louis Gai?"

"Once in a while, but never on tong business. He has a regular clientele, too. I've looked into a thing or two for him."

"Word also says you can keep a secret."

"The word *discreet* on my business card is not hyperbole."

"Good to know. The people I work for don't care for blabbermouths. I went into the military after college. Eventually became a Ranger. Rode on a lot of black ops in the sandy countries. Decided after two tours that I didn't care for military life, but when I got out, I only knew rugby, English literature, and killing. As personally enriching as it might be, there's no money in literature, and there aren't a lot of openings out there for rugby coaches. I got into a little trouble because of some head shit I was working through at the time. That put me in touch with people who worked for Mr. Bugliosi. I'm security, Gold. Like a bodyguard. When Mr. Bugliosi travels, he needs someone to watch his six. That's all I do. I don't come from the land of vino and vendetta, so they don't let me in on the juicy stuff. I'm not in on the rackets or the collections or anything else illegal. Most of that shit, I don't know anything about it. That's for serious. God's honest truth. Think of me the same way you would a Secret Service agent. My job is to hog bullets for the big guy if the black flag goes up."

"You'd do that?"

He banged a knuckle on his chest. I heard the dull thud of body armor. "Boy Scout motto. Be prepared."

"Could you walk away?"

He shrugged. "Maybe. Who knows? It's not like I'm carrying a lot of secrets inside my head. My job pays nicely. Nobody's taken a shot a me yet, and I've been doing this for a while. Tell you the truth, Mr. Bugliosi's business is about eighty percent legit these days."

"But that other twenty percent…"

"Best not discussed."

"You ever decide to take a walk on the mild side, give me a call. I can provide experience and supervision for you to earn your PI license."

"Why'd you do something like that for me?"

"Need one more merit badge to fill out my sash. But, let's get back to Lydia. What can you tell me about her?" I asked.

"Not much. I can tell you what she was like back in the day, but people change."

"You said she had daddy issues."

"That much was obvious. When I knew her, her father was already in prison, but according to Lydia he hadn't been much of a constant in her life before he was sent away."

"You know why he was in prison?"

"Something about an armed robbery. Armored car, right?"

"It was a big deal thirty years ago."

"Thirty years ago, I was reading Spiderman comic books and discovering masturbation. I didn't pay a lot of attention to crime news."

"He and some partners knocked over an armored car. Five went in, four were arrested."

"Everyone but this Eddie Rice character?"

"He was the wheelman. When the heist went south, he boogied with the cash. The others decided to shield him, in hopes they'd get their cut if they ever got out of prison."

"And you think Lydia ran off with Rice and the cash."

"I think her priorities leaned more toward the cash."

He took a sip from his coffee and stared out the window. "Yeah. I can see that. It would be like her."

"In what way?"

"Even back in high school, Lydia wanted everything right *now*. I don't think she ever heard the term *delayed gratification*. When she wanted something, she went for it, no holds barred. There was this chemistry teacher at school. Nice looking guy. Lovely family. She ruined his life. I wasn't there, you know, but the story went around. The guy went to his office for his planning period, sometime in midafternoon, and she was there, buck naked, sitting in his office chair. He told Lydia to beat it, but she threatened to scream rape if he didn't do exactly what she wanted. She was a teenager, and this guy was in his middle forties. Like I said. Daddy issues. He caved, and she talked anyway. Last I heard, his wife and kids moved back east, and he was living in a one-bedroom firetrap in San Bruno. Of course, that was a long time ago. For all I know, he was rehabilitated and went back to work for the schools, but I'm betting against it. Principals and school boards take a dim view of teachers putting it to their students, regardless of who started it."

"And no word from her you can recall?"

He wiped his mouth with a napkin, stared at me for a few seconds, and leaned in.

"Okay, sure. I saw her again. It was, maybe, three years after high school. I was home for the summer, and she called me up one night, asked if I wanted to come over to her place for a party. Her old man was in prison, and her mother worked double shifts to make ends meet, so she had people over all the time. Only, this time, she didn't tell me it was a party of two. She had some bone-shakin' weed. We watched some TV, and we made out some. She asked if I wanted to come up to her room. Fuck, Mr. Gold. I was twenty-one, had a woody like a flagpole twenty-three hours a day. Of course I said yes. Now, here's the weird thing. We start throwing down, and out of the blue she says, *'Hit me.'*"

"Hit me?" I asked.

"Yeah. Like it's nothing. I figure she wants a little of the old porn spanking. You know. Light playful stuff. So I slap her butt a couple of times, and she gets angry. Turns around and looks like she's super aggravated. She said, again, *'Hit me, damn it.'*. I couldn't figure it out at first, but then it all came together. She wanted me to really slap the shit out of her, and not her ass. Her face. I'll tell you, I been around the park a few times, but that was some freakin' weird shit."

"What did you do?"

He smiled. "I'm not proud about it, Gold. Sure. I played a little palm music on her. It really turned her on. Didn't do a damned thing for me, and in fact I don't think I handed in my best performance that night. Then she told me, the next time we got together, she wanted me to tie her up."

"How'd that work out?" I asked.

"I never saw her again. Looking back, I imagine I was so freaked out, I intentionally avoided her. Can't recall for certain, but I know we didn't hook up again that summer."

"Ever hear from her again?"

"No. If she reached out, I probably wouldn't answer anyway. My occupation notwithstanding, I work hard to keep people like Lydia out of my life. Who needs the aggravation?"

"Any idea who might know where she is?" I asked.

"Besides Maisie? Maybe. There was a guy. He was the equipment manager for the football team. I'm not talking him down, you know. I mean, he was a nice enough guy, but didn't have the build to be an athlete, so he did what he could. Can't recall his name right now, but he had a crush on her. I mean, he had it bad, man. The kind of crush that makes you whack off to her yearbook photo. I hear he got it on once or twice with Lydia. What was his name? Oh, yeah. Luke Whistler. I don't know what became of him, but he was living *la vida Lydia*—all Lydia, all the time. She was all he talked about."

"Thirty years is a long time to carry a torch. Any idea what became of Whistler?"

"Naw, man. I didn't keep up with any of the folks I knew back then. After spending several years dodging homicidal guys with pillowcases wrapped around their heads, the lives of a bunch of self-absorbed high school kids seemed trivial. No common frame of reference. I suppose I was too much an action junkie to stay in touch—I mean, what would we have to talk about?"

"I see what you mean," I said.

TWENTY-FOUR

The Summer of Love was a distant, indistinct memory, but remnants of a San Francisco's brief, tumultuous hippie era still linger in the Haight. One of them is a thrift boutique specializing in clothing from back in the day—hand-woven wool serapes, fringed suede boots, big floppy hats, the vestiges of America's lost generation. The sign out front called it The Natural Boutique.

Luke Whistler was tall and rail-thin, with a full beard that fell to mid-chest. His head was shaved, and he covered it with a multicolored wool beanie. He peered at me from behind round, indigo-colored lenses in his glasses.

"Private eye, huh?" he asked.

"Yep."

"Must be exciting."

"It has its moments."

"These days, a big night for me is getting blazed and listening to Pink Floyd while I watch Mandelbrot fractal zooms on YouTube."

"Yeah," I said, not entirely sure what he was talking about. "I'm trying to find Lydia Carlisle."

"Wow," he said. "That's a memory jog. I haven't thought about Lydia in years."

"Some of your classmates think you had a thing for her," I said.

"Sure I did. Lydia was hot. I mean, I know we aren't supposed to objectify women, but Mother Nature declared attraction is part of the package, right?"

"Sure," I said.

"I crushed on her pretty heavy, man. But I wasn't alone. There were a lot of geeky loner kids in school like me, and we all wanted five minutes in a dark closet alone with Lydia. I actually got it, though."

"Five minutes?"

"Seven. It was a party game. Seven Minutes in Heaven, they called it. Anyone tell you Lydia wanted to be an actress?"

"Not yet."

"She did. She was talented. I mean, she wasn't likely to win any Oscars, but for a high school kid, she wasn't bad. Problem was, she was always on, you know?"

"On what?"

"No, man. *On*, like on stage. She walked around like she expected everyone to watch her. Had to be the center of attention. And she liked to punk people."

"How?"

"Our high school drama director was a former hippie, the real thing. He lived just half a block from here when it was all going down in the sixties. He was still kind of weird when he was a teacher, pulled a lot of sketchy shit. Liked to get close to his students. I mean, like *really* close. Students used to hang out at his place on the weekends. He was single, and he had money, and he still had a lot of drug-dealing buddies here in the Haight, so every weekend was a nonstop party at his place. I hear he even slept with a couple of the students, including Lydia, but I never saw any of that. We were hanging there one weekend, and Lydia was pissed because we were doing *A Midsummer Night's Dream*, and she hadn't been cast in her dream role of Titania. She pitched a major hissy, crying and wailing and snot and tears running down her face. Then, in half a second, she turned it off. Looked around the room and said, *'Now, that's acting!'*, like she was showing the director what he could have had. She did that a lot. I think she could access fake emotion a lot better than the real thing, dig?"

"You said you got your seven minutes with her?"

"It was that same weekend. Maybe it was her disappointment at not getting the part she wanted, but she was on a tear. We played that Seven Minutes game. Deal was, you'd spin a bottle, and whoever that bottle pointed to got seven minutes in the closet with you. It was a pretty large closet, so there was plenty of room to roll around. After five or six rounds, it smelled pretty funky in there, too, but I was seventeen and mostly still a virgin. When she spun the bottle and it landed on me, I nearly creamed my jeans on the spot. Seems a little silly now, looking back on it, but I really had the hots for her. There were dozens of girls in my school who I know would have jumped my bones given the chance, but when you're seventeen you don't have an accurate perception of your own attractiveness, and you reach for the moon. I was an easy four, maybe a five in perfect light. Lydia was a freakin' ten, man. Maybe a Nigel Tufnel eleven. She was beautiful and hot and a little wild, and I just knew we were gonna rock the seismographs once we got inside the closet."

"Didn't work out that way?"

"At first, yeah. We closed the door, and she said, '*Okay, let's do this thing,*', and she stuck her tongue down my throat. I gotta tell you, Mr. Gold, it was intimidating. Then, just like she did with the crying jag, she flipped. One second she's licking my tonsils, and the next she pushed me away, sat in the corner, and rocked back and forth. I thought she was putting on an act again, so I played along. I sat next to her and rocked back and forth, just like she was. You ever hear the saying about people having fire in their eyes? That's what happened. She said I was making fun of her, and it wasn't fair, and then the waterworks started again. I couldn't tell what was acting and what was real. Longest damned seven minutes of my life. Funny thing. It didn't cure my Lydia jones. I replayed our time in the closet over and over in my head, trying to figure how I could have stopped her tailspin. After a while, I concluded I'd done something wrong. That was her way, man. She could make you feel like everything bad that happened was your fault. It bothered me for a long time, but eventually I got over it."

"Ever see her after high school?" I asked.

"Once in a while. People drift away. After a few years, I stopped thinking about her. I took a few classes in psychology in college, learned just enough to be dangerous. Realized she was the one with the problem, not me. Some kind of personality disorder. Maybe several of them. You know about her father?"

"I do."

"I think he fucked her up badly. When he got sent away, after the robbery, it really messed with her head."

"Another person said she had daddy issues," I said.

"It fits. I don't think she ever wanted to go inside that closet with me. I was way too young for her. There was this chemistry teacher at school…"

"I've heard the story," I said.

"You know he killed himself?" Whistler asked.

"No."

"About five years later. Sat on a cliff down near Half Moon Bay, stuck the loud end of a shotgun in his mouth and pulled the trigger with his toe. His whole life went sideways the day he walked into his office and found Lydia sitting in his chair. That's what she did to people, Mr. Gold. She was so self-absorbed, she never saw how she screwed up other people's lives. You know what, though?"

"What?"

"Years later, I'd still like another shot at that seven minutes. Go figure."

TWENTY-FIVE

Earleen Marley is a professor of psychology at San Francisco State University, and a former client. A few years ago, one of her students developed an unhealthy crush on her. The police couldn't do much about a stalker who denied following her around, so she turned to me. There's a longer story in here, but the short version is the kid doesn't bother her anymore, because he definitely never wants to see me in his life again.

I called Earleen after I dropped Heidi off at the gallery. She agreed to meet with me the next morning.

Her office was as orderly as her mind. Her desktop was nearly empty, save for a telephone and a picture of her fiancé.

"That's new," she said, pointing at my cane.

"Taking up parkour at my age was—in retrospect—not my smartest moment."

Her ebony skin and chestnut eyes glowed as she chuckled.

"Not gonna tell me, then," she said.

"What the hell?" I said. I told her. She laughed again. We both laughed. With the passage of time, I began to see the humor in my impalement.

"How can I help you?" she asked.

I told her what I had learned about Lydia so far, especially Clark Riesenberger's amateur diagnostic suggestion.

"Borderline personality disorder," she said. "It's a complicated diagnosis. I'm very interested in her fugue state during the encounter with this porn star."

"I think he was a porn star in training at the time. I understand he already had all the tools, though."

"Hung?"

"Heidi and I interviewed him yesterday at a shoot in Marin County. He was tanning nude. You know those snakes the Amazon? Anacondas?"

"White boy?" she asked.

"Yeah."

"Uh-huh," she said skeptically, drawing it out.

I pulled out my phone and did a search for Randy Bullcock. I handed the phone to Earleen. She took one look and handed it back.

"Walk proud, young man," she said. "Okay, so it looks like he is clearly qualified for his career."

"What's a fugue state?" I asked. "You said Lydia went into one just before we digressed into a discussion of freakish genitalia."

"The bit where she stared off into space and then started in with baby talk? It's like adult Lydia took a cigarette break, and she didn't recall what happened while she was gone. Not actually a fugue state in the classic sense. In true fugues, people have no idea who they are or how they got there. Lydia seemed to display an alter personality."

"You mean split personality? Like *Three Faces of Eve?*"

"I want to say *no*," she said. "But...maybe."

"Why the hesitation?"

"Because I don't believe in multiple personality disorder," she said. "The actual term nowadays is *dissociative identity disorder*, but it's the same thing. Very controversial diagnosis."

"How so?"

She rose to her full six feet and crossed her office to the bookshelf, from which she drew a volume bound in purple, and held it out to me. I flipped through the pages.

"The Diagnostic and Statistical Manual," she said. "The bible of diagnosis. This is the latest edition. It's updated every ten or fifteen years, to reflect the current understanding of clinical disorders. When the American Psychiatric Association workgroup on dissociative disorders were writing the criteria for DID, they were flooded with requests from practitioners across the country begging them to delete the entire category from the manual."

"Why?"

"You have to understand, Eamon. There is no such thing as monolithic psychiatry. There are a lot of little philosophical camps. Freudians, radical behaviorists, cognitive-behaviorists, humanists, neuropsychologists, and so on. None of them agree on what causes most disorders. The psychoanalytic camp—the followers of Freud and all the sons and daughters of Freud—ruled the organization for decades, but nobody becomes a psychoanalyst anymore. They're dying out, and they lose more of their power with each new edition. This last time, they were nearly outvoted. I strongly believe the next edition of the manual will delete the category entirely."

"But aren't people still diagnosed with multiple personalities?"

"Sure, by psychoanalysts. Nobody else touches the diagnosis. I'm in the cognitive-behavioral camp. We don't believe the disorder even exists. Your description of this Lydia chick, though…well, it makes me think."

"So what's the difference between borderline personality disorder and multiple personality disorder?"

"Man, you have opened a whole new can of controversy there. The very terms are confusing, since multiple personality disorder isn't a personality disorder at all. That's why they changed the name. It was confusing. Borderline personality disorder is very much a thing, I'm sad to say."

"Clark Riesenberger said he was in no position to diagnose her, but he did say that most women with borderline personality disorder were sexually abused."

"Categorically not true," Earleen said. "But a fair number were. I don't think it's a causal factor, but if a young girl or woman is unstable enough, sexual abuse could make matters worse. I don't trade in psychoanalytic unconscious mind claptrap myself. However, it is possible that Lydia's father abused her from an early age. Perhaps she learned that affecting little girl behavior dissuaded her father from carrying the abuse too far. You know what a chicken does with an ostrich egg?"

"No."

"It tries to hatch it. It's called a supernormal response. So, Lydia starts to have sex with Captain Firehose, and that triggers her fears of being abused. To protect herself, she reverts to a conditioned infantile state. It's only temporary, though. Can't say for sure why she snapped out of it."

"Everything I've heard suggests that Lydia was overly dramatic."

"A symptom of borderline personality disorder. Extremely dramatic behavior is common in the population.

When they think they are being abandoned, they can revert to manipulative behaviors to keep the person attached."

"Lydia was abandoned by her father when he went to prison. She became promiscuous and mentally unstable afterward."

"I think she was mentally unstable all along," Earleen said. "Being *abandoned* by her father only exacerbated the symptoms."

"Clark moved to Los Angeles for college."

"Which may have helped trigger the bizarre personality change. She could easily have seen him leaving for another city as abject abandonment. Beyond that, Eamon, I'm deep in the land of speculation. Tell you what, though. I can't diagnose Lydia across time and space, but I can say what I'd want to rule out first. I think your Lydia is a sick little chicken. You may never find her. The suicide rate among woman with BPD is very high. Those who don't kill themselves often lead highly self-destructive lives and die young as a result. You may be looking for a dead girl."

TWENTY-SIX

I was running shy on leads. Luke Whistler hadn't come up with any more names of people to interview. I could have given Clark Riesenberger another call, but my impression was he traveled in much different circles than most of his high school class, Maisie Duncan being the exception. Maisie was another possibility. With the benefit of time, perhaps she had remembered some other people I might bulldog.

But, for the moment, I was back to tracing Eddie Rice. My leg had healed sufficiently to allow me to drive, so I hopped across the Bay Bridge and joined the eastward clot of travelers on I-580 toward Modesto.

According to CyberShamus, Eddie Rice lived in Modesto when he was twelve, before he was sent off to eat state food until he was old enough to vote. His last recorded public school was Prescott Junior High. I discovered long ago that school yearbooks are great places to find information. Since the adult Eddie Rice was out of reach, I went in search of Eddie the Kid.

Prescott Junior High looked like the unfortunate offspring of a one-night stand between a used car lot and a for-profit prison. A blocky central two-story main building was surrounded by squat single-story classroom pods. All the buildings were painted in Caribbean white, with anodized metal roofs. Being near the middle of the Central Valley, the terrain lay flat as a lithography stone and extended to the horizon in every direction. It reminded me why I almost never visit Modesto.

An attractive black woman in her middle thirties attended the front desk. The tag on her breast announced her as Catprice Hight. I handed her one of my cards.

"A private detective? Those are for real?" she asked, her eyes wide. "I thought they were only on television."

"I'm real, and they aren't," I said. "Catprice?"

She chuckled, in that well-practiced way people do after answering the same stupid question a couple thousand times. "Short version? The *'t'* is silent. I blame my parents. But doesn't everyone? Don't ask. Guess that's a dumb thing to say to a private eye, huh?"

I'm looking for information on a student—"

"I'm sorry, Mr. Gold, but we can't release any student-related information. It's a federal law."

"How about a student who was here fifty years ago, and probably died years before that federal law was written?"

"For real?" She seemed overly concerned about reality.

"Well, I'm not certain about the 'dead' part, but he was definitely here fifty-one years ago, as a seventh-grader. I don't think he lasted out the entire year before getting carted off to juvie for the rest of his adolescence. This kid would have made a big splash back then. I just want to see if there are any residual ripples."

"I don't know if I can help you. There's nobody here now who worked here fifty years ago. I don't even think the records from those days are still available. We have only a limited amount of space for storage." She leaned forward. "Want to know a big secret?"

I leaned in. "What?"

"You remember all those times your teachers told you one thing or another was going in your permanent record?"

"Yes."

She looked both ways, as if checking whether anyone was eavesdropping, and then said, "There is no permanent record."

"Go on."

She smiled as if she had just divulged the contents of Area 51. Personally, I thought she had spent far too much time in the company of teenagers, but her smile melted my heart. I liked Catprice Hight.

"What would be the point? We keep records on admissions, classes, grades, and graduations. That's it. There's something called a 'confidential folder', which sometimes contains more sensitive information, but it's destroyed a few years after high school graduation. So, even if we could find any records on your possibly dead student, I don't think they'd tell you much. Especially if he left before the end of his first year here."

"How about a yearbook? How far back do you keep them?"

"All the way. They have their own shelf in the school library."

"Do you think I could get a look at the annual for the year this student attended?"

"Security is very tight here. You'll need an escort."

I gave her the smile I use to cajole IRS agents during audits.

"Are you volunteering?" I asked.

"If it gets me out of this office for a half hour. Follow me."

I hobbled on my cane behind her. On the way to the library, she said, "What happened to your leg? Old war injury?"

"Horrible Red Rover accident. You don't want to hear the gory details."

"Do you carry a gun?"

"Sorry to disappoint. I'm not strapped today. It's a junior high. How dangerous could it be?"

"You been asleep for a decade or two? Just as well. We don't allow guns on campus. I watch a lot of old detective shows on TV. You know. *Peter Gunn. 77 Sunset Strip.* They all carry guns."

"I rarely need one, and they're kind of hassle to carry around. You ever try to sit down to dinner with a milk carton stuffed up under your arm?"

"No, but I'm the adventurous sort. I'll give it a try."

"So, *Peter Gunn* and Kookie, huh? You ever watch anything made after 1960?"

She gave me the smile again. "I really like black on white stuff, you know?"

She might have winked, but if she did it was at slightly less than the speed of light. I probably imagined it.

"You mean black *and* white?"

"Sure, I do. Here's the library." She held the door open, so I walked through. "Yearbooks are in the back-left corner. Might be dusty. Nobody ever goes back there. I'll show you."

She touched my arm gently to guide me., but I could feel the tension in her fingers. She was right. The back stacks were a paper graveyard. Piles of magazines dating back years bowed the metal shelves. Outdated encyclopedias, moldering reference books, obsolete texts, and, at the very back wall, a sagging wooden bookcase containing row after row of yellowing, dust-encased yearbooks. The mélange of decay and mildew that draws bibliophiles to antique stores everywhere hung in the air and made my sinuses itch. I was surprised mushrooms didn't grow in the corner.

"See what I mean?" Catprice said. "You could stash a body back here. You ever stash a body, Mr. Gold?"

"I'm the guy who catches guys who stash bodies. Remember?" I said absently, as I drew a finger along the spines of the yearbooks, looking for the right year. I lied, of course. I had stashed a body or two in my time, most recently at Corona Farms in Sonoma, but I don't discuss it.

"Which year?" Catprice asked. I told her. She found it in seconds and held it out to me as if presenting a royal newborn. I tucked it under my arm, just as she stepped on an errant volume of The Encyclopedia Americana—1950s edition—and lost her balance, falling into me. The yearbook dropped to the floor as she tumbled, and I grabbed her to break her fall. Her hand fell against my chest as she braced herself and lingered there.

"Still looking for a gun?" I asked, wincing as the injury to my leg strained with the effort.

She pulled away and straightened her skirt. "Lucky you were here to catch me."

"Ms. Hight, I believe you are flirting with me."

"I'm flirtatious by nature. My single flaw. Is it working?"

" *'There was another life that I might have had, but I am having this one.'* "

"Kazuo Ishiguro? An educated private eye?"

"I read a lot on stakeouts. But that wasn't the intended takeaway."

"Taken, huh?" she said, her eyes betraying only the slightest hint of disappointment.

"Not exactly. But I'm also not *not* taken. We're still working it out."

"It's complicated," she said. She pulled closer to me, her lips inches from mine. Her eyes narrowed; her pupils dilated.

It would be so easy.

I thought about it and nodded. "Complicated enough already. But let's say you've made my day. Let's find some light, so I can look at this yearbook."

We hacked our way out of the dead paper stacks and found a red oak table in the reading area. I took a chair at the head, with Catprice next to me at the corner.

"The kid's name is Eddie Rice," I said. "He would be in the seventh grade."

I riffled through the pages until I found the student pictures. Seconds later, we located Eddie Rice. The photo showed a gap-toothed sandy blonde boy with deep blue eyes and a shy smile.

"Not a bad looking kid," Catprice said. "What'd he do?"

"Robbed an armored car. Killed a cop. Ran off with twenty million dollars."

"No shit."

I glanced at her.

" *This* kid?" she asked, jabbing at the picture with her fingernail.

"I'm sure Hitler took a damn fine baby picture," I said. "Is there a copier nearby?"

"Why do you need his picture?"

"I don't have one."

"But this kid is twelve years old. It was half a century ago. He looks a little different now."

"I have a friend at Berkeley," I said. "Woman I did some work for a few years back. She's conducting some spectacular research with age progression in photographs, the kind of stuff they use to update photos of missing kids on milk cartons, but on steroids. Between you and me, I think she plans to market a phone app and retire as a millionaire. More power to her. I'll ask her to age young Edward here to about sixty-five, and then we can put a face to his name."

"You do a lot of this?"

"Finding people? All the time."

TWENTY-SEVEN

I had worn out a lot of shoe leather, and the sum total of my investigation yielded mostly this: Lydia Carlisle was a head case, and Eddie Rice was a cypher.

The round trip to Modesto had taken most of the day, with a stop in Berkeley to drop off Eddie Rice's junior high school picture with my friend there. Her name was Barbara Ledford. She was a middle-aged petite force of nature with short dark hair and eyes that saw more colors than the average bear. Literally. She had some genetic condition that enabled her to distinguish between extremely minute frequency changes in light compared to normal people. For most of her early life, she had presumed that everyone could see millions of different colors. When she discovered she was gifted, it instilled a desire to know more about vision and how it works. That was her grocery-buying gig. The age-progression software she had developed was moonlighting.

She took one look at the picture I had brought her, and said, "I don't know, Eamon. This is really old. Offset printing back in the day used rubylith technology. Think computer pixels, only a lot larger. This photo is one inch by one inch. If I blow it up to a usable size, all you'll see are huge dots."

"But you have a workaround," I said.

"I always have a workaround. It will take a while, though, and I'm afraid it may negatively impact the resolution of your picture. What we'll do is, basically, fill in the blanks between the dots with some predictive technology software. Then, when I blow it up, at least it will have some continuity. Unfortunately, it will likely look like you photographed the kid through gauze."

"I could still use that."

"Hold your horses, Cisco," she said, smiling. "A colleague is working on image-sharpening programs. He owes me a favor, and he's kind of sweet on me. He's a kid, only in his late twenties, but I won't hold that against him. If I ask him to enhance the image, he'll do it within an hour."

Now, I waited. Like I said, this age progression business is a sideline for Barbara. She had other duties that commanded the lion's share of her time. She'd told me it might be several days before she could render a usable image. I didn't see that as a horrible deal.

By the time I arrived back from Modesto, my leg throbbed and ached. Saving Catprice from falling in the stacks had aggravated matters. I took a naproxen, chased it with a nice Kolsch from a local brewery, and sat in my recliner overlooking the Bay to think. All the running around looking for Lydia Carlisle and Eddie Rice had taken a toll on me, in my recovering state. As I considered what move to make next, I dozed off in my chair.

An hour or so later, I felt a blanket settle over my body, and I smelled the faint wisp of Heidi's aroma. I opened my eyes. She had settled on the sofa to read a magazine. When I turned my head to her, she looked up.

"Is it worth it?" she asked.

"What?"

"You should be on vacation, recuperating. Instead, you're dashing from pillar to post chasing people who probably died a quarter century ago. You still make my toes curl, lover, but if I'm being brutally honest, I have to remind you. You're no spring chicken. Take a break. Why don't we head down to the Montara house for the weekend? You can fiddle with that thingamajig you're building."

"The hurdy-gurdy," I said.

"Yeah. That. Get your head away from armored car robberies and dead guys and missing daughters and probably unrecoverable millions. We'll eat and drink and drink some more, and if you're really nice, there may be canoodling."

I gazed out the window, as lights came on at the tourist piers, and fog started to flow lava-like over Mount Tam. I sighed.

"You had me at canoodling," I said.

Heidi, as usual, was right. We decamped to Montara and hung out for the weekend, doing not much of anything that had anything to do with Eddie Rice and Lydia Carlisle.

On Sunday, I had a Forty-Niners game on the television, the sound turned low so Heidi could concentrate on the novel she read while lounging on the sofa. I kept busy working on the hurdy-gurdy I'd promised a friend in Colorado. What he wanted with a hurdy-gurdy was hard to fathom, but I was the only guy he knew with the knowledge and skills to build one—my first—so I threw myself in with vigor. I did take more frequent breaks than usual, because standing for extended periods of time on my healing leg became uncomfortable. The breaks offered opportunities for that canoodling Heidi had portended.

A hurdy-gurdy is a monstrosity of an instrument, sort of a Frankenstein noisemaker constructed from parts of a violin, mountain dulcimer, autoharp, and bagpipes. The sound is akin to playing a cheap violin while someone strangles a cat in the background. You don't pluck it or bow it. Instead, you crank it, and a wooden rosin-coated wheel rubs against the strings like a violin bow, continuously. Several of the strings can be tuned using keys, like an autoharp, but several are drone strings, which moan underneath the melody like a neglected spirit. It's an immensely complex instrument, with little tolerance for error, so naturally I quaffed a few brews before settling in to work on it.

I was in the early stages. The hardest part was finding good plans, until a friend directed me to The Guild of American Luthiers, who sold them on their website. In this session, I only planned to join the two halves of the back of the instrument, and the two halves of the front. The main body was to be constructed from walnut, for no particular reason except that I like the way it smells when I work it— spicy and sweet, kind of like the sound it made. The top would be close-grained old growth European Engelmann spruce I'd ordered at considerable expense. I don't scrimp on the materials in my instruments.

I selected a nice six-inch wide board of wildly figured California claro walnut. The grain ran through it like oily tsunami waves. I stood it on its side and sliced it into two halves on my bandsaw, and then repeated the process with a thick slab of the spruce. This allowed me to lay the two halves side by side, like opening a book—in fact, the process is called *bookmatching*—to create a symmetrical mirror image. I planed them to thickness, raising a bit of a sweat in the process.

The next step was to stack the two halves of the back, face to face, and joint them. There are expensive electric tools for doing this, but I find them noisy and aggravating. I get perfect results using a shooting board, in which the stacked halves of the back are clamped in place between two perfectly flat-sided boards, with only a millimeter or two exposed to the air, and the jointing edges are formed using a keenly honed hand plane tipped on its side. A few quick *snicks* with the plane, and the mating surfaces were perfectly flat and ready to glue.

While the glue dried on the joined back, I repeated the process on the spruce top. It was nowhere near as satisfying, since spruce doesn't smell much like anything when you work it, but I did revel in that moment when I popped the two halves out of the shooting board, held the edges together in front of the window, and not a speck of light pierced the joint. It was a good stopping place.

Heidi sensed it as well.

"Hey, Pops, take a load off," she said from the sofa. I was all too happy to comply. First, though, I poured us a couple of glasses of a nice Argentine Malbec. She put the book away and we listened to barely audible rumble of waves on the beach across the PCH. Steaks marinated in the kitchen, and in a bit I'd light the charcoal in the grill. For now, though, we relaxed and talked about everything but my case, until Heidi broached the subject.

"Any closer?" she asked. She didn't need to say more.

Richard Helms

"Maybe. Maybe not. Tell you the truth, I don't think I'm going to find Lydia Carlisle. I think she's buried somewhere, under a name she never owned, and has been for a long time. I consulted with Earleen Marley after I talked with all of Lydia's old beaus."

"Earleen? The psychologist?"

"Yeah."

"I like her."

"She's a peach. She also thinks Lydia might be—or was—a genuine psycho ward case. She tossed around terms like *multiple personality* and *borderline*. Intimated Lydia was the 'live fast, die young, leave a haggard, drug-soaked and STD-riddled corpse behind' type."

"Oh," Heidi said.

"You have a frame of reference?"

"I knew a few of those in my youth."

"You're so adorable when you talk like you're old."

"Years and mileage," she said, wistfully. And she was right. What she lacked in years, she had compensated for with decades of life experience. I was the only person in her life who knew Heidi had grown up under a different name—one to which even I wasn't privy—and how she lived under peril of retaliation from German anarchistic terror cells should they every discover her new identity. Fortunately, thanks to the machinations of her late father, a former high muckety-muck in the German security services, she was hidden under layers of carefully constructed red herrings even I couldn't fathom. The price had been staggering. She was cut off, forever, from everyone she had known and loved before she became Heidi Fluhr. I frequently lay awake at night, wondering how I'd bear up under that loss.

"So, what do you think?" I asked. "Am I chasing a ghost?"

"You're doing what you do," she said. "You didn't ask Abner Carlisle to walk into your office. When he was killed, you asked the next question. And the one after that. You're kind of obsessive that way. Obsessions are hard to shake."

"You think I'm acting pathologically?"

"Sometimes obsessions are good. Look at Michelangelo. But, yeah. Sometimes you get a whiff and can't resist following the scent to its source. I just hope, this time, it isn't rotting."

TWENTY-EIGHT

I spent most of Monday in my office, deliberating whether it was worth my time to pursue Lydia Carlisle. I'd stacked a ton of billable hours on Jackson Pike's account already and had dug up almost nothing except a tale of a pitiable, desperately lost young woman who was almost certainly dead. It had rained heavily all day. The steady cadence of drops beating against my office window lulled me into drowsiness. The downpour and the fog that accompanied it completely obscured the bay. I could hear the occasional honk or bleat from the sea lions on rocks near the bay shore, but most of them had sought shelter from the weather.

Two sets of footsteps resonated on the stairs, and I checked my Browning before stowing it inside the drawer of my desk, easily concealed but readily available. I didn't expect any trouble, but it was a habit. As Sonny Malehala had noted, be prepared.

Steve Gaddy and Jasper Durante walked through my door. Their full-length coats were drenched from shoulder to breast. Both wore SFPD ball caps to keep their heads dry.

"Parking's a bitch around here," Gaddy said.

"Thought cops could park anywhere they want," I said, sliding the drawer closed.

"Sure, if there's a space. You'd think the rain would drive the tourists away."

"Hell," I said. "Even earthquakes don't drive them away. Here to ask about Riley Quinch?"

"Naw." Gaddy took a seat across from me. Durante remained standing. It was an old cop intimidation trick. One does the talking while the other looms and maybe putters around examining objects in the room. Gaddy removed a picture from his pocket and slid it across my desk. It was an old mug shot.

"Recognize this fellow?" he asked.

I glanced at the photo. Someone named Louis Francis Canizzaro, according to the placard he held.

"Never heard of him," I said.

"He's a made guy. One of Stan Pistone's thugs."

I knew Stan Pistone. He was a *capo* running one of JuneBug's crews out of the area south of Market. Like, way south. Think Daly City. It was difficult to imagine that bland, boring, cookie-cutter-community-by-the-sea as a hotbed of mob activity, but I suppose wiseguys of one type or another are everywhere these days. You gotta love the land of free enterprise.

"What about him?" I asked.

"Interesting case of mistaken identity. The M.E. was piled up all week. Some tong violence down in Chinatown produced a bumper crop of autopsies, so it took him a while to get around to the Abner Carlisle case. Imagine his surprise when we ran the prints he pulled from the body..."

"And it wasn't Carlisle," I said.

"You know anything about this?"

"I know how to add two and two. Louis Canizzaro was the body in Carlisle's hotel room?"

"Prints don't lie," Durante said.

"This is curious," I said.

"How so?" Gaddy asked.

"This is the second contact I've had with one of JuneBug's guys recently. I interviewed one of his bodyguards yesterday. Fellow named Sonny Malehala."

Gaddy scratched at his chin. "I hope you aren't working the Carlisle case. It's an active murder investigation."

"I couldn't care less about Carlisle," I said. "At least, not until now. I'm working on recovering the take from the armored car robbery, and in the course of that I was hired to find the Carlisle's daughter, who probably ran off with Eddie Rice."

"The wheelman," Gaddy said.

"Yeah. But the whole Eddie Rice thing is ancillary. I'm only interested in the money and the girl."

"It's all one big headache now," Gaddy said. "What have you found so far?"

"Bunch of nothing. I tracked down Eddie Rice's mother. She hasn't seen her son in decades, but she's in a ritzy retirement home she can't afford, and according to my source there her bills are paid regularly. Leads me to believe Eddie Rice is still alive and kicking."

"Did it occur to you he might have tried to kill Abner Carlisle and got this Canizzaro instead?"

"Sure, but like I said, I wasn't interested in the Carlisle deal. I told you guys about Rice last week. I figured you were looking for him too, but that was none of my affair." I tapped the picture. "This changes things. If Carlisle is still alive, he's also looking for Rice and his daughter."

"And, he's our prime suspect for the murder of Lou Canizzaro," Gaddy said.

"Yeah," I said. "That too."

TWENTY-NINE

Heidi and I lounged under a blanket at her apartment. We had TCM on the television, but the sound was down. Heidi was much more engrossed in my search for Lydia Carlisle and the missing money. She was particularly interested in my news about Abner Carlisle.

"He shouldn't be hard to find," she said.

"How do you figure?"

"He's whiter than the underside of a flounder. He's like a walking ghost. Guy like that stands out in a crowd."

"Maybe he's gone to ground somewhere. It would be the healthiest thing to do. The dead guy in his hotel room was a thug named Canizzaro, works for one of JuneBug's crew bosses."

We had been together long enough that she was familiar with JuneBug. I felt her shudder under the blanket. "Someday you need to take a job that doesn't put you in dutch with gangsters."

"A consummation devoutly to be wished."

She poked at me. "You joke, but I know better. That deal at Corona Farms last year bent you so bad, you were months getting straight. My advice? Ditch this spec job you're doing and find a wayward husband or something."

"I met one of JuneBug's watchdogs already. Assured him I wasn't trespassing on their turf. Just before I learned Carlisle was still alive, I was seriously considering dropping the case. Now, Carlisle might be looking for Rice and Lydia too, and if he is, we're likely to cross paths."

"Poor Lydia," she said. "I feel for her. She got a really shitty deal."

"I suppose she did. She didn't ask to be born to an abusive criminal. Her mother's wound a little tight on the bobbin, too, but she earned it the hard way, supporting Lydia on two jobs for years. Something about the way her friends from high school describe her, though, makes me wonder whether we aren't fated to madness at birth. There's something to be said for the old nature/nurture problem. Is the fault in our stars, or in ourselves? I suspect Lydia would have been a handful even if she had been born into a family of saints. There were some serious demons jostling for space inside her head."

"Now you know the father's alive, what's your next move?"

"I'll drive to Mill Valley tomorrow and let Jackson Pike know his wife's first husband is still breathing. It bothers me that Carlisle's wandering around, probably also looking for Rice. My motive is money. Carlisle wants to put Rice in a box. If he finds out where his ex-wife is, it could mean trouble for her and Pike. Better if I find Carlisle first. I'm not likely to do that if I drop the Lydia case. I might call around tomorrow to the other PIs in the city, see if Carlisle's been in touch since his supposed demise."

"And if you run across him?"

"Steve Gaddy and the entire SFPD are on the lookout for him over this Canizzaro murder. If we meet up, I'll drop a dime on him. Kill two birds with one stone."

She snuggled in closer, taking care not to jostle my leg, which ached badly as it healed. "You are a poor liar," she said. "One of my favorite qualities in a man."

THIRTY

I expected Joan to answer the door the next morning, but Jackson Pike opened it instead. He had a cell phone in his hand.

"Mr. Gold!"

"Is your wife home?" I asked.

"No. She has a ladies' club each week. She left about an hour ago. Is this about Lydia?"

"I'm afraid not. May I come in?"

He opened the door wider and escorted me down the hall to his office. It was lined with rich walnut wainscoting and lit several table lamps with forest green glass shades. The furniture was fine leather, and the center of the room was dominated by a claro walnut desk. As a woodworker, I approved. He gestured for me to have a seat and returned to his call.

"Sorry, Gene. Go back to what you were saying...And the shortage is...That much...I don't know what to say. I may have an idea, though...Tell Harlan I'll call him in about an hour...Yeah...Call me if you hear anything else."

He thumbed the phone dead and placed it on his desk.

"So sorry. I was on a call when you rang the bell. Can I get you a drink? Some tea? A cola?" he asked.

"Don't want to trouble you."

"No trouble at all. It's a drive from the city, especially this time of the morning."

"Well, a Coke if you have one. Or ginger ale."

"Be right back."

He hustled out of the room, leaving me to inspect his private domain. The walls were festooned with photographs. Pike with a former gap-toothed governor. Pike standing next to an oil derrick. A picture of Jack and Joan Pike standing in the middle of the X in a skydiving target, their deflated chutes billowing behind them. One picture piqued my curiosity. It was a photo of a racing car, sliding sideways on a banked dirt track corner. A window net hid the driver from view, but the photographer had caught the name 'Jack Pike' painted on the roof over the driver's side window

"I was hoping to hear from you," he said as he returned. He handed me a can of cola and circled the desk to his chair.

"Why's that?" I asked.

"A couple of reasons. First, why are you here?"

"Maybe it's a good thing your wife isn't around. I have some news you might want to ease in on her. Abner Carlisle isn't dead."

He collapsed back in his chair and cocked his head. "I... I don't understand."

"The body found in his hotel room the other day wasn't his."

"Who was it?"

"A hood named Canizzaro. Works for a gangster in the city named Junius Bugliosi."

"I've heard that name," Pike said.

"He's an old-time mobster, but most of his enterprises these days are legitimate. He sometimes moves in select circles, if the police aren't putting too much heat on. I saw your picture with the governor. I hear he had a picture of himself with Bugliosi somewhere in the state house. You might have run into him around town."

"I doubt that. But your description of the man worries me. If the fellow found in Abner's room worked for this gangster, does that mean there's a connection to Joan's daughter?"

"I don't know. I'm still getting my head around the idea Carlisle isn't dead. That's why I came today. I checked every other private cop in town. Carlisle hasn't contacted any of them. But it's only a matter of time before he tracks down your wife. When he does, he'll probably show up here. The police detective running the case is keeping the news about Carlisle under wraps. Nobody gives two craps about a dead ex-con in a hotel room anyway, so if he does come to your door, treat him with kid gloves. He's not interested in you. He wants this guy Rice and your stepdaughter. And the money. Give him whatever information he wants and call the police as soon as he leaves. If you like, I could set up a stakeout to keep an eye out for him."

"That... that won't be necessary," Pike said. "I have some security people who work for my company. I can retask them to watch the house. In fact, as I said, I'm glad you dropped by. That telephone call was from one of my construction managers, with a company I diversified into a few years back. It's a small commercial construction firm. We build strip malls and the like. Toss 'em up quick and cheap and charge an arm and a leg per square foot. It's amazingly profitable. Anyway, my manager says someone's stealing from us. Building materials are disappearing at an alarming rate."

"What kind of materials?"

"The expensive stuff. Copper wiring, fuse boxes, power tools. Someone made off with a pallet of bricks a few nights ago. A whole fucking pallet of bricks! They had to use a forklift just to load it up. What really worries me, though, is someone tried to break into a locker where we keep detcord."

"I don't know what that is," I said.

"It's explosive. We don't keep a lot around, but it's sometimes useful if we run across entrenched roots or rocks while grading the properties. It's safer than dynamite, but it still packs a huge wallop. According to Gene, the explosives locker was tampered with. If the detcord was stolen, it would be a big deal. The feds are kind of touchy about loose explosives. We keep thirty feet of it in the locker."

"What could you do with thirty feet of this detcord?"

"Make a hell of a mess. Could hurt people nearby if it goes off. It's pretty stable—much more than dynamite, but you don't want to fuck around with it. So, you can see my concern."

"These security guys you mentioned. Don't they provide you with night watches?"

"They're not that kind of security. They're not rent-a-cops. They're more for personal protection."

"I didn't know the oil business was so dangerous."

"Being wealthy is dangerous these days, Gold. Kidnappings are not unheard of. Man has to protect himself."

"You look like you can take care of yourself."

"One on one? Without weapons? I can hold my own. Get beyond punching and biting and clawing, add a second bad guy or two, and I am in the land without hope."

"Got into a lot of fights in your wildcatting days?"

"Believe it or not, no," he replied. He showed me the race car photo hanging on his wall. "It was that same time, though. When I was young, I thought I'd live forever. Did anything dangerous I could find. Skydiving, roughnecking, did a little rodeo bull riding because it turned the chicks on. For a brief time, I drove race cars—mostly dirt jalopies. It was cheap and fun, and once in a while it got my pulse pounding. I bet we had five or six knock-down drag-out fights in the pits each week. One guy I recall went after another with a pipe wrench one night. Never really knew why. Got myself into a tussle or two. Some people can't leave it out on the track."

"You're an adrenaline junkie," I said.

"Was. That was decades ago. These days, the most exciting thing I do is get out of bed in the morning. Making it through another night's something to celebrate. About these thefts. Would it be too much of an inconvenience to pull you off the Lydia thing for a few days? Aubrey Innes says you're as good as they get when it comes to industrial security. Says you plugged a huge hole in his business."

"Why not call the cops?"

"I've been doing this for a long time, Mr. Gold. First sign of blue uniforms, and the thief will go to ground. It looks like an inside job. One of my employees may be stealing from me. I want to know who it is. Once you figure that out, you can be sure I'll call the police on him. You get the evidence, and I'll handle the rest."

THIRTY-ONE

Pike had christened the construction business China Clipper Builders, a play on the *'China Clipper calling Alameda'* quote from the old movie. The business was housed in a commerce park in Alameda, across the bay. The manager was named Harlan Bolt. He was middle-aged and robust, his skin sunbaked to leather. He introduced me to Gene Haake, China Clipper's head of security.

"It's more an honorary title," Haake explained as we toured the site. He was average height, but slim and loose, like a taller man. "I'm a construction estimator by trade. Harlan and I are among only five full-time employees here. The rest we hire by the job. It's a gig economy these days. No point in paying people if there isn't any work. Mr. Pike asked if I'd like to be head of security along with my other duties. Gave me a hefty bonus to take the job. Between you and me, I don't know what I'm doing. I check the locks and make sure the place is secure at night, and still stuff goes missing. Bought us a couple of dogs we leave loose inside the building with the expensive stuff overnight, and I put in a couple of closed-circuit cameras here and there, but with all the thefts lately, I think I'm in over my head."

"The cameras didn't show anything getting stolen?" I asked.

"Nothing. I can show you the recordings. I'm not saying these thieves are slick or nothing, because—like I said—this whole security thing is new to me. Mr. Pike told Harlan you do this sort of thing for a living. I figure we can use all the help we can get."

"Do you have an inventory of all the items that have disappeared?"

"In my office. It's strange. Mostly piddling stuff—some power tools, a pallet of bricks here or there, a generator or two. Someone lifted one of those big site radios we use to play music during construction."

"Mr. Pike mentioned the thieves tried to steal some detcord," I said. "What can you tell me about it?"

"Whoever pinches that stuff had better be careful," Haake said. "Detcord is dangerous stuff. I mean, you can whack it with a hammer and toss it off a roof all day without it going off, but under the right conditions a piece about six inches long could kill a man if it exploded in his hands."

"What is it, exactly?"

"What it says. It's a cord, about half an inch thick. You know the fuses on firecrackers and skyrockets?"

"Yeah."

"Detcord looks sort of like that, only thicker. When you get right down to it, it's just a long fuse filled with plastic explosive, but it burns at an incredible rate, faster than any fuse. About three miles a second."

"You said three *miles?*"

"More than that, to be exact. About sixty-four hundred yards. Burns so fast, it looks like the whole thing explodes. Made out of a chemical called PETN. I don't know the whole scientific name for the stuff, but it's nasty. We keep it

171

under lock and key in Building Four over there. Don't want it sneaking out, because you could do a lot of damage with it, and it's federally controlled. A thirty-foot length of detcord could be concealed in your pants, though I don't think I'd like to walk around with that kind of firepower so close to my junk, you know?"

"So, somebody could walk in, stow thirty feet of detcord in a grocery bag, and walk out without being noticed?"

"Sure. Of course, they'd have to get in first. That's what worries us. Like I said, there are only five full-time employees here. I'm no expert, but I can't find any sign that the lock on Building Four has been forced or jimmied, which means this might be an inside job."

"Mr. Pike thought the same thing. Show me Building Four."

I followed him across the complex. Like the other structures, Building Four was a World War II era domed Quonset hut, made of corrugated steel attached to a metal frame. The door slid on creaky hinges, secured by a massive padlock.

"First problem," I said as I examined the door. "Doesn't have anything to do with your thefts, but I could probably bend this hasp off with my bare hands. It's old and weather-worn. The lock is fine, but it's attached to a flimsy piece of metal. Might want to replace the hasp or invest in more secure doors."

He unlocked the door and slid it to one side. The interior of the hut was dark and musty. It smelled like freshly-poured concrete. I peered inside but could only see gloom and indistinct shapes.

"Got a camera on this door?" I asked.

"Sort of. I only installed two cameras, so I placed them where they could see the largest portion of the work yard. One is halfway up that pole there—" he pointed to an electrical pole on the other side of the yard. "The other covers the parking area."

"Need more cameras," I said.

"We're counting on you to tell us how many and where to put them."

"We'll get to that. Show me inside."

Haake flipped a switch, and three ceiling-mounted fluorescent lamps buzzed to life. At first the illumination was weak, but as the lamps grew steadily brighter, objects in the building came into focus.

"We keep the detcord in this locker," Haake said, pointing toward a stamped-metal box secured by a cheaper padlock. He unlocked it and threw the locker open. Inside were three boxes labeled DANGER: HIGH EXPLOSIVE, and the manufacturer's name for the contents. Haake opened one of the boxes to show me. A look of mixed horror and consternation crossed his face as he withdrew his hand.

"Dear God," he said. "It's missing."

THIRTY-TWO

"I don't mind telling you, Mr. Gold. This puts me in a tough situation," Jackson Pike told me after driving across the bay to join us at China Clipper Builders. "The feds are gonna be up my ass over this."

I had spent the hour since Haake found the empty detcord box in the locker policing the perimeter of the storage building. I had just finished when Pike pulled up in his Caddy. We showed him the empty box from the locker.

"What I've found isn't going to make you happier," I said. "Come with me."

I led him outside the hut, and around the back. Behind a stack of rotting wooden pallets, I showed him an area where the thin steel shell of the Quonset had been pulled away, leaving an opening just large enough for an adult man to shimmy through.

"They cut their way in?" Pike asked.

"I don't think so," I said. "At least, not recently. This opening has been here for some time. Look how the edges have rusted. Any thief who doesn't take care could walk away with a nasty case of lockjaw. My guess is, someone knew about this breach already, and exploited it."

"Why not go in through the front door?" Pike asked. "You told Gene you could rip the hasp off with your bare hands."

I pointed to the pole-mounted camera that swept the yard. "They didn't want to be famous. At first, I thought it might be an inside job. Someone had to know where you'd placed the cameras, and what their field of view is. Then, Mr. Haake showed me the camera images inside the main office. I could see the fronts of all the buildings, but almost anyone could get around to the back undetected."

"But the lock on the explosives storage locker..." Pike said.

"Yeah, about that. Come with me." I led him back inside Building Four, to the explosives locker. I held up the lock that had fastened it.

"Cheap piece of garbage," I said. "You put your best lock on the outside door. It's a quality piece of equipment securing a swiss cheese hasp. This lock is trash. Any schoolkid could crack it. I wouldn't trust it to keep my shit safe in the Y locker room."

I pushed the shank into the lock and spun the dial. Within a minute, I had it open again.

"Your combination is 34-26-9."

"That's right," Gene Haake said.

"Yes," Pike said. "Clearly, Mr. Gold, you are the right man for this job."

"Oh, I can help you with your security problems going forward," I said. "And I'll charge you handsomely for it. This, though—" I gestured toward the locker. "This is between you and the feds. Thirty feet of high explosive is on the streets tonight because you cheaped out on storing it. I can't help you with that. The guys down at ATF would resent my interference."

"And I will report it, immediately," Pike said. "There'll be hell to pay, but you're right. I'm at fault. Guess I'll have to take the woodshed time on it."

I was surprised. I wasn't used to rich people shouldering the blame for their transgressions. I had expected Pike to lay the blame off on Haake, let him take the heat. Instead, as the owner of China Clipper Building, he figured the buck stopped with him. I grudgingly liked Jackson Pike.

"If you'd prefer," I said, "I can set up a stakeout for the rest of the night, until your employees show up tomorrow morning. After I grab a little shuteye, I can come back and assess your security needs."

"Yes," Pike said. "I'd appreciate that. If you'll excuse me, I have to make some telephone calls."

I sat in the front seat of my car all night, except when I made an hourly patrol of the yard. Nobody attacked me. Nobody climbed the fence to storm the explosives hut. The Clue Fairy never showed her face.

The first workers arrived an hour after sunrise. None of them approached the hut. Jackson Pike's Caddy still sat outside the main office, so I thought I'd stretch my legs and pay him a visit.

He sat behind his desk, holding a cup of coffee. His desktop was littered with folders.

"I called ATF," he said, before I could even greet him. "They're sending a couple of investigators later this morning. Surprisingly, they didn't sound terribly concerned. So I did some research. Do you have any idea how much high explosive material disappears each year?"

"Is this a pop quiz?"

"I didn't know either. A lot. I read five different accounts of missing dynamite, TNT, PETN, and detcord just over the last six months. What in hell do you think people are doing with this shit?"

"Who knows? Terrorism comes to mind, but it isn't as if we see attacks by homegrown bombers every other week. Maybe it's just rednecks lighting off sticks of dynamite and chucking them into a rock quarry. What they might do with detcord is beyond my limited imagination. Wanted to let you know I'm off the clock. Headed home for a nap."

"Before you go," Pike said. "Tell me straight up. Do you think this is an inside job? Is one of my employees stealing from me?"

"Can't eliminate the possibility. Whoever copped your explosives knew about the breach in the hut. Suggests they've been here a lot. Have you dealt with the ATF before?"

"Not over a theft."

"Believe me, they'll drag every one of your employees over the coals. If it's an inside job, they'll find out."

"But you could you still work the case. Discreetly, I mean?"

"Mr. Pike, I'll take every penny you want to throw at me, but I'll sleep better giving you the hot poop and straight skinny up front. You don't need me for this. The feds will do a thorough investigation, and they'll hand off part of the case to local police who'll look for the missing detcord. I'd just get in the way and piss off people who specialize in this for a living. I'm better used trying to find Lydia."

"Yes," Pike said. "I see. As it happens, I planned to call you this morning in any case, even before the detcord went missing. You want some coffee?"

He crossed the office to the coffee maker to freshen his cup. At the rate he was pounding it back, they'd have to peel him off the ceiling by lunch. I deferred. He prepped the cup with sugar and creamer, and returned to his desk, where he cradled the cup between his hands. He watched the swirls of cream revolve around the rim.

"It's a hard thing to learn your spouse is keeping secrets," he said.

"I can imagine," I said.

"Ever been married?"

"I flirted with it once or twice, but never bit the hook."

"Have anyone special?"

"There's someone I like better than anyone else. Beyond that, we don't examine it closely."

"Suppose you found out she had lied to you?"

"I did. I discovered she wasn't who she said she was. She had assumed an entirely new identity, for good reason."

"Sounds like an interesting story."

"One I'll never tell. The word *discreet* on my business cards also applies to my private life."

"Were you disappointed when you found out?"

"No. But I'm a tough guy. I'm used to surprises. What did your wife lie about?"

He opened a drawer and pulled out a short pile of letters tied together by a stout rubber band. He slid them across the desk to me.

"I came home last night and found my wife crying in the kitchen. As you might guess, we've talked a lot about Lydia over the last several days. Your visit opened barely healed scars. It turns out you were right. Lydia did contact Joan after she disappeared. She wrote several letters."

I riffled through the letters. There were eight of them. The postmarks covered roughly six months and were from different cities.

"She stopped writing?" I said.

"Joan answered the last letter. It was a shot in the dark, considering it looked as if Lydia was moving around, and frequently. According to Joan, she had reached the end of her rope. She said some things in her last letter that could be seen as...hurtful. She never received another letter from Lydia. No phone calls, either. When no more letters arrived, Joan blamed herself. She believed she had driven her daughter away with her words. She carried that guilt for over a quarter century, Mr. Gold. It took a lot for her to admit it."

"Yes."

He picked up a folder. "I scanned and printed the letters and the envelopes. It's all in this folder. I'm sure you can understand that Joan doesn't want to let the actual letters out of our possession."

"Of course."

"About the letters, Gold. I've read through them. None of them mentions this Eddie Rice you're chasing. Lydia doesn't mention traveling with a companion at all."

"Interesting," I said.

"Is it possible Carlisle was wrong? Maybe Eddie Rice disappearing and Lydia running away was a coincidence."

"I don't like coincidences," I said.

"But, if it is, then chasing after Rice isn't getting us closer to Lydia."

I took the folder from him. "Rice is all I have. And, if Carlisle was wrong, then I'll hit a dead end and have to start over. Maybe something in the letters will give me a new trail to follow. I'll look them over later this afternoon, after I grab some sleep. While I kept watch last night, I made some notes regarding your security arrangements here. I'll put together a list of recommendations over the next day or so, and we can go over them then. We good?"

"Absolutely. Get some rest. At least one of us should be alert."

THIRTY-THREE

It was one of those dreary, sleepy autumn days on the San Francisco Bay, the sky dark and low, wind whipping off the water and driving clouds of briny mist across my office windows. I couldn't make out the tops of the Golden Gate Bridge spires in the muck. A few hundred feet away, sea lions lazed on pilings and rocks. The weather affected them as it did me. They scarcely bothered to trumpet as the spray enveloped them like wispy smoke. It was a day for a fireplace and a good book, but some of us have bills to pay.

I had spent the morning reading the letters Lydia Carlisle had written to her mother a quarter century earlier, which probably contributed to my foul mood. The people who knew Lydia best had painted a consistent and vivid picture of a wanton, uncontrolled, rebellious hoyden. The letters reinforced the image. Lydia had alternately cajoled and excoriated her mother. Letters that began pleading forgiveness frequently ended with recriminations and name-calling.

I pictured Joan Carlisle, before Jack Pike came into her life, waiting each day for the postman to drop off the mail, hoping—regardless of what scalpel-edged words it contained—there would be a new letter from her runaway daughter. Then I imagined her reading the letters I'd examined, and how they must have flayed her heart into ribbons. No wonder she had kept them a secret from her new husband. The letters betrayed a rancor between mother and daughter that would send most bachelors running. Who wants to sign on for a lifetime of refereeing the Fight of the Week?

I'd only met Joan once, but I'm pretty good at sizing people up. She was brittle and life-weary, but I didn't see in her the harridan that Lydia depicted in her letters. If I were a practitioner of the psychological arts, I might conjecture any number of parent-child dynamics that could explode in rage, accusations, and even physical threats. For all I knew, Joan and her daughter fed off each other, polar opposite personalities that sustained a perpetual attraction and repulsion controlled only by the gravity of their genes.

The letters also gave me insight into Joan Carlisle. From a skewed perspective, Lydia's rage toward her mother might have been justified. The pathological relationship between Lydia and Abner couldn't have passed unnoticed. By the time she was an adult, Lydia understood the degree to which Joan had strategically ignored the abomination taking place under her roof, and she wasn't about to let her mother off the hook. Joan, for her part, must have wallowed in guilt. She'd kicked the can as far down the road as it would go, and now the can was kicking back.

The letters were fucking depressing. Parenthood was not yet a complete irrationality for me, but the letters I'd read that morning were no recommendation for it.

Pike was right. None of the letters mentioned a traveling companion at all. No reference to Eddie Rice in any way. That bothered me. If Carlisle only imagined his daughter had run off with Rice, with no real evidence to support it, then I was on the wrong track. My two cases might have diverged again.

The damp gloom made my leg throb. I considered closing up shop and taking Heidi to lunch, but I heard footsteps on the stairs leading to my office door. Seconds later, someone rapped on it.

"Entre vous!" I summoned exactly one eighth of all the French I recall from high school.

The door opened, and a man peeked around the jamb. He was heavy and thick. His jowls made his face a trapezoid, skinny end high. His eyes looked confused.

"Mister...Gold?"

"Oui!" I said. Another sixteenth of my remaining French expended.

"The door says *Eamon Gold, Discreet Investigations.* You're...*that* Mr. Gold?"

"The very same. Come on in. Pop a squat."

He was dressed in a rumpled but expensive suit, over which he wore a classic London Fog overcoat. There were sparkles of water in his curly pewter hair. He wore thick glasses, apparently for far-sightedness based on how they magnified his eyes.

"I spoke with you several days ago," he said. He slid a card across my desk. *John Rascoe.*

"With the armored car company," I said. "You enlightened me as to the true amount of money taken in the heist thirty years ago."

I stood, balancing myself on my cane as I shook his hand.

"Work-related injury?" he said, pointing toward the cane.

"They told me I could leap tall buildings with a single bound," I said. "They never told me how to land."

"Yes. I see. I probably should have telephoned before coming, but I didn't... actually plan to see you today. I was in the area, and I knew your office was nearby, so I decided to seize the opportunity as it were."

"The opportunity for what?"

"To satisfy my curiosity, mostly. When you called the other day, I had almost forgotten about the armored car robbery."

"If you don't mind me asking," I said, "What's your interest? The robbery was thirty years ago. Unless there's a horrific portrait in your attic, I can't imagine you were working at the armored car company back then."

"I was a young teenager," he said. "I lived four blocks away from the scene of the robbery. I heard the gunfire through my bedroom window. I stood outside the police lines and watched the investigators process the crime scene. I became sort of obsessed with the case. Followed the trials in the newspapers and on TV. Years later, after college and business school, and completely by chance, I wound up working for the bank. The two were unrelated, but I can't help thinking the robbery had something to do with attracting me to apply for the job."

"As the twig is bent," I said.

"I brought this." He opened his briefcase and handed over a thick file folder. I flipped through it quickly and whistled.

"This is the internal bank file on the robbery," I said. "How'd you get it?"

"My supervisor," he said. "I told him you had called, and you were looking at recovering some of the proceeds of the heist. He said I could give you the file. He's a kid, twenty years younger than me. Just out of Wharton. He doesn't give three fucks about a robbery that took place when his mom was a virgin."

I looked over the contents again. "I can keep this?"

"It's a loaner," Rascoe said. "*Quid pro quo*, you might say."

"*You* might."

"It's my buy-in. I already told you I was fascinated by the case. You might say it shaped my entire adult life. Even so, I haven't thought about it in years. Figured the last thief, Carlisle, would die behind bars. Things happened. Life stacked itself, and the heist became a neglected file in the back of a cabinet in my office. Since you called, I've thought of little else. I know you're doing this job on spec. I'd appreciate it if you'd keep me informed, in return for the file."

"Seems fair," I said. "Here's what I know. There was a sixth robber named Eddie Rice. He was the wheelman, so he hung back in a stepvan waiting for the rest of the gang to deliver the money."

"A stepvan?"

"They weren't knocking over a mom-and-pop liquor store. They needed a vehicle roughly the size of the armored truck. Twenty million in cash is not only bulky, it's heavy. So you need a big truck. Three-quarter ton at least. One ton would be better. A stepvan meets the qualifications, and there are thousands of them around the Bay Area. Makes a perfect getaway car. Might even have been a rental. Nobody notices a U-Haul on the highway. They loaded the cash onto the stepvan, and Rice took off seconds before the cops arrived."

"And this sixth person, the wheelman? Rice? What became of him?"

"Good question. He disappeared about twenty-five years ago, with the missing cash, and possibly Abner Carlisle's daughter. Jury's still out on that one."

"You don't say. No honor among thieves, I suppose. But, you're wrong. Rice wasn't the last man."

"Carlisle told me about him, himself."

"Oh, I'm sure he was in on the armored truck job, Mr. Gold. The money went *somewhere*, after all. But there was another person as well. A seventh man." He tapped the folder I'd laid on my desk. "Officer Petter."

"The cop who was killed?"

"Read the file," Rascoe said. "It's the result of the bank's internal investigation. They spared no expense— understandably, considering the amount of money stolen. They didn't release the information on Petter, out of respect for his family. They did give the information to the cops, but nothing ever came of it. Yeah. Petter was dirty as shit. But I'm intrigued by this man Rice, and Carlisle's daughter. No trace of them at all?"

"Like they hopped the off-planet shuttle. Their social security numbers are a dead end. No census records, no tax records. For all I know, they're in a shallow grave somewhere, and someone else took the money."

"But you're looking."

"It's what I do. The trail's cold, though. If they're still breathing, they've had almost a quarter century to build lives under new names. There are over three hundred million people in the United States. That's a lot of suspects to comb through, presuming they aren't living on a grape vineyard in the south of France. If they're expats, I'll probably never find them."

"You're taking on a lot of work for someone who doesn't have a paying client," Rascoe said.

"I'm bucks-up right now. I can afford to do spec work for a while. There may come a point when I have to back-burner the armored car case."

"The folder will help," he said. He stood and grabbed his overcoat from the rack. "My card's clipped to the inside cover. I really would appreciate it if you'd keep me in the loop. You can photocopy anything you want. Let me know when you're finished with it, and I'll pick it up."

THIRTY-FOUR

It was too nasty outside to walk to lunch, so I ordered burgers from the Buena Vista on Hyde Street and invited Heidi to trudge up the stairs for an intimate *le dejeuner*. I was rapidly running out of high school French words.

"New client?" she asked, as she slathered her fries with catsup.

"The guy in the overcoat? Nah. He works for the armored car company. The heist is kind of a hobby. He brought me a folder containing the bank's investigation into the robbery. All in all, this has been a fruitful day for clues. The girl's stepfather found a trove of letters Lydia Carlisle wrote to her mother after she ran off with Eddie Rice."

"And the money."

"And the money. Joan Carlisle didn't tell her husband Lydia had written. She squirreled the letters away twenty-five years ago and never spoke about them to anyone."

"Why?"

"Guilt, I suppose. Joan traded her daughter's childhood for security. She allowed Abner Carlisle to abuse Lydia, and after Abner went to prison Joan thought she could redeem herself through martyrdom. It didn't take. Lydia was already too broken. Joan blamed herself for driving her daughter away for good. She responded to the last letter with unkind words. She never heard from Lydia again. I've glanced over the letters she did receive."

"Any insights?"

"I still need to read them in depth, but the letters reinforce everything I've learned about the girl. The tone is rebellious. The language is provocative. Lydia Carlisle was basically that chick you dearly wish you hadn't met at a party. Beyond that?" I shrugged and chomped off a bite of the burger. It was juicy and tangy and salty and sweet all at once. A dribble of catsup rolled down my chin. I caught it with the napkin. "The postal cancellations are interesting. I ordered the letters by dates. Started off in Jackson Hole, Wyoming. From there, she went to Denver, and then Flint, Milwaukee, Chicago, and Minneapolis. That was the last one."

"What does that suggest?"

"They were moving around. Not putting down roots. Never staying in one place for more than a few weeks."

"Acting like fugitives."

"Eddie certainly *was* one. Only nobody knew it. Curious though."

"What?"

"Lydia disappeared over a quarter century ago. Carlisle always suspected she ran off with Rice, but he never fingered his silent partner in the heist. He never called the cops and said, 'Hey, guys, if you want to find out where the money went, I can turn you on to the man who took it.' Instead, he stewed in twenty-three hour a day solitary for over two decades, waiting to get out so he could go after Rice himself."

"And?"

"What does that tell us about Carlisle's values?"

Heidi dredged a fry in catsup and chewed on it. "His daughter wasn't as important as the money. Your friend Carlisle is a piece of work."

"Career criminals frequently are," I said, and chomped down on a hefty percentage of my burger.

"What about the bank investigation?"

"Haven't had time to digest it. The guy who delivered it—fellow named Rascoe—did leave me with one important piece of information. The cop killed during the shootout at the robbery thirty years ago was dirty. He was in on it."

"And his partners killed him?"

"Maybe they were covering their tracks. Maybe Petter was expendable, and it was always in the cards to kill him. Maybe he grew a pair and decided to stop the robbery. Who knows? If Abner Carlisle shows up, maybe I'll ask him. I might head across the bay to Sausalito and have another talk with Ellis Rhys."

"Who?"

"Ex-cop. He was Walt Petter's training officer. Thought the kid walked on water, or at least that's how he came off the last time we talked."

"You think he knows stuff he didn't tell you?"

"From the way he talked, Petter was like a second son to him. Maybe Rhys had no idea the kid was dirty. Maybe he's whitewashing his memories of the Petter because he knew all along. Won't know unless I ask. After lunch, I'll attack the letters and the files, and draft a list of questions. We'll see where we are then."

THIRTY-FIVE

"Had a feeling I'd see you again," Ellis Rhys said.

I'd called ahead. He had suggested I drop by his house, a Craftsman cottage with a deep front porch, on a hill overlooking the bay. Rhys lounged in a rocking chair. I took a wicker chair next to him.

"Lie to a cop, even a private one, and it will come back to bite you. You know that."

"Sure I do. Maybe I didn't give you enough credit, Gold."

There was no way to ease into it. "Your boy Petter was dirty," I said.

"And?"

"And…" I stopped. What had I expected? Immediately, the answer came. "He learned at the feet of a master."

"What are you saying?"

"You were his training officer. You were ready to put Abner Carlisle and his buddies up against a wall for killing him. The kid meant something to you."

"He wasn't a kid by then. But, yeah. He meant something. Wally was a great earner."

And it fell into place.

"He was part of your downline."

"And I was part of someone else's downline. Wally was workin' his own downline. I took a cut off Wally. Someone else took a cut off me. And so on, and so on. Jesus, Gold, I'm surprised it took you this long to catch on. You have any idea what a house like this in Sausalito costs these days? With this view of the bay? How many retired cops you know can afford a place like this on a pension and Uncle Sugar's geezer handouts?"

"What can you tell me about the armored car job?"

"What do you want to know?"

"Were you involved? Statute of limitations has run out. You can tell me anything you want and nobody can touch you."

"Fuck," he said. "Getting a beer. You want one?"

"Sure."

He returned moments later and handed me a bottle.

"I knew it was goin' down," he said. "Beyond that, I wasn't involved. Wally told me about it. The holdup gang needed him to turn a blind eye. That was all. They'd already planned where to hijack the armored car, and it was on Wally's patrol beat. All Wally had to do was be somewhere else. It was supposed to go smooth and simple. Nobody was going to get hurt. I knew Wally. I think I know what happened."

"What was that?"

"He couldn't resist getting a look at the robbery going down. He had the stupid bad luck to run over a bottle and was stranded with a flat tire in view of the entire holdup. Put him in a hell of a spot. Put the heist crew in a worse one. Even if he was outnumbered five-to-one, he would have to call in the robbery to dispatch. The gang didn't have a choice. Their shield was tarnished. On the off chance he might cave and call for backup, they had to kill him. He thought he was one of the boys, but they killed him anyway. Never even drew his weapon—did you know that? He probably got out of his car, approached the guys to see how to handle things, and took two in the chest and one in the leg. They didn't even give him the chance to fight his way out. That's why I wanted to execute the bastards. I was ready to do it, too. Hardest decision I ever made on the job. Splashing those asswipes would have ensured Wally's name was never tarnished. They came within seconds of being hamburger."

"You buried the report from the armored car company."

"Least I could do."

"I'm confused," I said. "From what I can tell, Abner Carlisle and his gang were a bunch of losers. They couldn't plan a decent birthday party. And they weren't from Sacramento. How did they know to approach Petter? How'd they know he'd have his hand out?"

"Now you're asking the right questions," Rhys said. "You tell me, Gold. Who knows every cop on the beat willing to get greased?"

"People who regularly pay cops off. Career criminals. Mobsters. Are you saying the mob bankrolled this heist? Because I have the bank's official inquiry records, and they never implicated any organized crime figures."

"They never told anyone about Wally, either. Wonder why."

"They had their sacrificial lamb," I said, after thinking about it. "They knew insurance would reimburse the entire take. Outing a crooked cop might only delay the payback.

Saying it was a gangland robbery would draw too much attention, and also push back reimbursement. They fashioned a story that made sense and spiked the facts. The documents they provided made it obvious Petter was complicit. They kept it a secret."

"And got paid," Rhys added.

"It all comes down to getting paid, doesn't it?"

"In more ways than you know," Rhys said.

"What do you mean?"

"Way I see it, things went one of two ways. Your wheelman—what's his name?"

"Eddie Rice."

"Yeah, Rice. In one scenario, he bolts with the money just as his buddies are lacing Wally up. He takes the money to the guys who actually planned the robbery, they eliminate the last loose end and leave the gang hanging."

"Doesn't flush. Rice visited Abner Carlisle in prison after the trial. If the mob murdered him, they took the long way around."

"Then there's the other scenario. Rice saw the robbery going south, so he ran with the money. He went into hiding, only surfacing to visit his buddies in prison. Who knows? Maybe the mob didn't know everyone on the armored car job. Maybe they don't know Rice's name. The holdup guys in prison kept his name a secret in hopes he'd mother-hen their cuts until they were released. The mob is still waiting for their end of the heist."

"If you hadn't been dirty, you'd have made a hell of a detective," I said.

"I *was* a hell of a detective. Want to see my collar percentages? I put a lot more bad people away than I let get away with shit. City wants squeaky-clean cops, they should pay us better."

"Oh, shit," I said.

"What?"

"I met with one of JuneBug's security guys the other day. He knew Abner Carlisle's daughter in high school. I hoped he might have a lead to her whereabouts."

"Did you mention this wheelman, Rice?"

"Yeah. I did. The guy didn't know the name."

"Doesn't mean he didn't memorize it. If he took it back to JuneBug…"

"It would be the first break the mob has had in finding the money since the robbery."

Rhys leaned back in his seat and took a long drag from his bottle.

"Never met a made guy with a short memory. Know what I think?" he asked.

"What?"

"You and Carlisle might not be the only people looking for Eddie Rice now."

THIRTY-SIX

Jackson Pike wasn't pleased with my news.

"With the mob possibly involved," I said. "The risk to you and your wife just went up. I'm as sorry as I can be, but when I talked to this Malehala guy the other day, I didn't know his boss probably underwrote the armored car heist. I shouldn't have told him Eddie Rice's name, but again…"

"You didn't know. If you knew how the cards were stacked in a deck, you'd probably never gamble. I'm not worried about myself, but you may be right about Joan. Perhaps she should take a little trip, at least until this whole mess blows over."

"What about you?"

"Can't. Not right now. This explosives business with the feds. Wouldn't look good if I suddenly left town. Don't worry, Mr. Gold, I can take care of myself. The bounty of a misspent youth. I know how to fight dirty."

"With all due respect, the mob specializes in that, and they have a lot more practice."

"The matter's settled. I heard from Mr. Haake. He told me he received your recommendations and guidelines for improving security at our Alameda work yard."

"It will be expensive, but should end the kind of problems you're having with the feds right now."

"I appreciate your quick work on it."

"The bill's in the mail. Parcel post."

"I'm sure your report is worth every penny. I'm still concerned about the possibility that the detcord theft might have been pulled off by one of my own employees."

"I ran background queries on all of them while working on the security report. They all checked out. Clean as a whistle. Hardly more than a traffic ticket between them. I could be wrong, but that weighs against an inside job. Perhaps one of your contractors—"

"It's not important. Certainly nothing for you to worry about. It's the ATF's problem now, right?"

"And yours."

"Which is why I'm so grateful for your security report, Mr. Gold. I've weathered far worse in my time, and—as you noted—the new security system should prevent recurrences. Thank you again. I'm afraid our meeting will be necessarily brief. I need to make travel arrangements for my wife."

I had just returned to my office when my cell phone buzzed. Kevin Krantz at the *Chronicle*.

"What the fuck are you investigating, Eamon?" he asked, almost before I said hello.

"Say again?"

"North End Investments." The name of the company paying for Calliope Rice's nursing home.

"You found it?" I asked.

"It's a pass-through holding company, registered in Delaware." he said.

"Delaware?"

"Delaware has the loosest corporate laws in the country. Check the back of every credit card you own, and you'll find the company is located there. It's like corporate nirvana."

"Explain this like I'm stupid," I said.

"North End is a shell. It has only one purpose. It's a money conduit. Money comes in, money goes out. That's all it does, and unless I miss my guess, it's all done automatically by some computer somewhere. You aren't going to find any offices or clerical workers. As far as I can tell, the sole purpose of North End Investments is to pay the nursing home bills for this woman you interviewed. But that's not the interesting thing."

"What is?"

"Pass-throughs are usually established to avoid paying corporate taxes."

"They're a dodge."

"Exactly. Have you considered incorporating, Eamon?"

"Why on earth would I do that?"

"Enormous tax advantages, to begin with. Owners of pass-through corporations pay individual income taxes, but the corporation has no tax liability."

"Still don't see the advantage."

"It's a huge one, if you can't identify the owners."

"In which case nobody pays any taxes," I surmised.

"It's a shelter," Kevin added. "It's intended to help reduce the potential of double taxation for the really hugely monetarily endowed, but in this case the owners aren't flesh-

and-blood humans. Every one of the corporate shareholders in North End Investments is also a corporation."

"Oh, boy," I said. "And, when you tracked back those corporate owners..."

"Who says I did that?"

"I know you. You tracked them back."

"Well, yeah, but I don't want to be predictable. And, by the way, for this job you owe me a hell of a lot more than a bottle of scotch and an Alexander's steak. I spent days on this."

"So, spill it."

"North End Investments is part of a network of shell companies so vast...well, I don't think I've ever seen something this convoluted. North End is listed as being owned by three corporate entities—Hopsewee Limited, Orange Mango Lines, and Tempe Consolidated."

"Tempe Consolidated what?"

"It doesn't matter. Want to guess why?"

"It's a pass-through also?"

"I don't know why everybody in college called you dumb. None of the three entities seems to do anything except—"

"—funnel money," I finished.

"You're getting it. And when I investigate all three companies—you want to jump on my punchline again?"

"They were owned by other companies, none of which had a human principle owner."

"I tracked this web back fifteen generations. I never found the name of an actual human being. After a while, names started reappearing. I'm willing to bet somebody has constructed a network of corporate shells arranged something like the intersections on a chessboard. Every company owns part of another somewhere along the line. It's the most incestuous business model I've ever seen."

"Meaning what, exactly?"

"Someone doesn't want to be famous," he said.

"Underworld types?"

"Maybe. I hear the CIA does this sort of thing, too. They use it to set up covert front organizations without divulging their funding is coming from you and me."

"And nobody in college called me dumb. Lazy, drunk, and horny? Maybe. I'd like a look at that structure."

"I'll email you the spreadsheets and the inconceivably Byzantine flowcharts I built over the last several days. Good luck untangling it. When all is said and done, though, I think it's wasted effort. Somebody made a lot of effort to become invisible."

THIRTY-SEVEN

I spent the rest of the day trying to make sense of the Gordian knot of data Kevin attached to his email. He was right. The list folded in on itself so many times, it could have been a Cirque de Soleil act.

In the end, I gave up. Whoever was paying for Calliope Rice's nursing care—and I still maintained it had to be Eddie Rice, dead or alive—didn't want to be found. It was one more dead end in the deadest end of a case I'd ever encountered.

But what did I expect? I was tracking down people who disappeared without a trace decades ago. They had a massive head start on me.

I looked over the labyrinthine list of shell companies again, and one of them jumped out at me. *Atlas Controls.* For some reason, it was familiar, but I couldn't place where I'd seen it before. A quick Internet search yielded nothing. According to Kevin, like the other entities on the list, not a single individual human was listed on the shareholders list. Nothing separating it from the other companies Kevin had unearthed, but for some reason it struck a chord. I had seen it *somewhere.*

After trying to find it in my increasingly overwhelmed head for a quarter hour or so, I decided to give it a rest and concentrate on something else. You can think too hard about some things, and as a result never locate them. I turned the radio to a local jazz station and leaned my chair back to rest my eyes.

I jerked back upright several minutes later as footsteps echoed up the stairway to my office. I opened my office drawer, and quickly berated myself for leaving my Colt Python in the gun safe bolted in the trunk of my car. The most dangerous weapon at my disposal was a letter opener.

Someone knocked on my door three times before twisting the knob and walking through. I relaxed. It was Sonny Malehala. Then I tensed again. He held a Glock automatic at his side.

"There!" I exclaimed. "Never fails. When you can't figure out what to do next, have a guy burst into the room with a gun."

"You gotta come with me," he said, mechanically.

"Thought you were just a bodyguard. When did you graduate to muscle?" I asked.

Malehala's face didn't even twitch. "I'm sorry, Gold," he said. "This isn't my call."

I reached for the letter opener. He was faster than I would have thought, and before my fingers even touched it, he had his pistol leveled at my nose.

"Please, don't," he said. "Not on my account. Mr. Pistone would like a meeting."

"I don't see him here," I said.

"Because he doesn't want to meet you here. Duh. Like I said, I'm sorry. Mr. Bugliosi pays me nicely. I may not agree with everything he does, but I do respect his power, and I like the life he's given me. Because I owe him, I told him about our meet the other day. I...I didn't know."

"You didn't know that Bugliosi contracted the armored car hit thirty years ago?"

Malehala blinked, twice. "You know about that?"

"Figured it out only yesterday. Beyond that, I can't think of a shred of information I have that would be of the slightest interest to JuneBug..."

Malehala scowled, and his finger slipped inside the trigger guard. I held up both hands.

"Right. Got it. *Mr. Bugliosi.* Beyond knowing he engineered a heist thirty years ago, I know about as much as you do. This case has been nothing but dead ends."

"Then you have nothing to worry about. My car's downstairs. You'll need a jacket."

I considered giving Heidi the high sign as Malehala walked me out to the street, but I didn't see her behind her desk through the glass gallery door. Just as well. Probably wouldn't pay to deal her in on my personal horror show anyway. I didn't think Stan Pistone meant to make me disappear, but I'd spent enough time in the presence of gangsters to know he didn't call me out on a rainy San Francisco day to discuss the resurgent Forty-Niners. He was going to throw some weight around. My job was to be duly impressed, possibly visibly intimidated, and to answer any questions he had honestly. Professional hoods know lies better than anyone. If I tried to toss a zinger by Pistone, I was likely to spend eternity in the trunk of a crushed '73 Monte Carlo at the bottom of a flooded quarry.

Malehala drove. I sat in the passenger seat watching the worn windshield wipers smear road grime around on the glass.

"Did you give Maisie a call?" I asked.

He ignored me and concentrated on driving. I pulled my cell from my pocket and dialed Steve Gaddy's number at SFPD. It went straight to voicemail, as I expected.

"Hi, Steve. This is Gold," I recorded. "I'm in car with a man named Sonny Malehala, who's taking me to an unplanned meeting with Stan Pistone. Since you're looking for Abner Carlisle, and I suspect this has something to do with him, I just wanted you to know, in case I should, like—you know—disappear or something. All right then. Thanks." I slipped the phone back in my pocket and smiled at Malehala, who scowled back. "Insurance."

"That wasn't smart," Malehala said.

"And getting in a car with a guy who's dragging me to see a major gangster—at gunpoint! —without telling anyone *is?*"

"Who was that? On the phone. Another private eye?"

"Public one. SFPD Inspector."

"Shit," Malehala growled. "You're gonna get me in a lot of trouble."

"I didn't start it."

"The cops are gonna hassle Mr. Pistone, and I'll catch hell for it."

"Relax. They were going to hassle him anyway."

"How so?"

"Guy from the armored car company gave me the internal investigation report. June—" Sonny glared at me. "—sorry. *Mr. Bugliosi* was strongly implicated. The cop they killed—Petter? Dirty. His former boss, also dirty, told me the mob backed the robbery and bribed Petter to look the other way. In those days, 'the mob' meant Mr. Bugliosi. But he only did Big Picture stuff. He greenlit operations, and underlings ran them. My guess is Stan Pistone was in charge of the robbery."

"And?"

"Just telling you how I figured out Mr. Bugliosi was involved. That tied Bugliosi to Abner Carlisle. Nobody cares about the robbery. It's ancient history. But someone killed one of Pistone's made guys in Abner Carlisle's hotel room, and the police care about that a lot. So, we reset the clock. Now the police are interested in the robbery as motive."

"You told them?"

"I haven't, but I was going to. Knowing Mr. Bugliosi organized the robbery didn't help me a bit, and I like my license too much to risk a withholding evidence beef. Inspector Gaddy's no fool. When he gets the message, he'll make the connection. Mr. Pistone was going to be hassled either way. You snitched me out, Sonny? Really? I thought we had a connection."

"You think I got within ten yards of you without first clearing it with my boss? He knew I was meeting you. I told you. Damn it, Gold. You put me in a hell of a spot. Wish to hell I'd never heard of Lydia Carlisle."

"I'm beginning to feel the same way. Where are we going, anyway?"

THIRTY-EIGHT

We drove across the bridge into Marin County, and from there into the hills surrounding Mount Tam. I had a lot of time to think through my options. There weren't many. I was miles from home, on the wrong side of the Golden Gate, and weaponless.

I was relatively certain I'd sleep in my own bed that night. The phone call to Steve Gaddy ensured that. On the other hand, I don't think anyone except me would give a damn if Pistone had me roughed up a little. My job was to talk my way out of it.

Civilization thinned, until it consisted of only the occasional inn or roadside craft shop, and then it disappeared entirely as Sonny hung a left onto a winding gravel drive lined with towering redwoods. I saw lights through the massive trunks ahead, near the crest of a ridge overlooking the Bay. We broke through the trees into a natural pasture about a quarter mile across, just below the ridge that rose above the treeline. An ostentatious log lodge stood at the edge of the pasture before it yielded to the scarf of the mountain. Light shone in the windows, and a curl of ash-gray smoke wafted from a great stone chimney.

Two men stood on the deep redwood deck and watched as Sonny pulled into a circular gravel drive and parked at the base of steep wooden steps. Both men were armed with FN

P90 machine guns, the kind the Secret Service uses, and I had no doubt they were illegally modded for full auto. The men looked confident. Confident is good when you're slinging a weapon that can spew nine hundred rounds a minute. It's bad if you're the guy they're pointing it at.

Sonny opened my door and held out his hand.

"Thanks," I said. "I can get out on my own."

"Your phone, asshole," Sonny said. "You've done enough damage already."

I handed him my phone, and he directed me up the steep stairs to the gallery. The two men watched me ascend, motionless as Dobermans at heel, until I reached the top. One shouldered his weapon and said, "Assume the position."

After a frisking that I found rather unnecessarily intimate—but had the good manners not to say so—Sonny escorted me through the front door. The main hall was the kind of place I'd expect to find Count Orloff. Hunting trophies hung on every wall—wild boar, deer, antelope, a couple of species I knew were on endangered lists, and one imposing moose. The place smelled like a blanket chest—aromatic cedar and age. The walls were polished heart pine, the floors red oak covered with enormous wool Navajo rugs. Spruce timbers, divested of their bark and gleaming under several coats of lacquer, made up the post-and-beam construction.

Befitting the lodge, the furniture was rough-hewn pine and forest-green leather, the upholstery sporting just the right degree of craquelure to qualify as fashionably vintage, but not yet shopworn or shabby.

Two men sat in rustic chairs near the fireplace. I didn't know the first one. He was short, no more than five and half feet, and built like a cinder block nuclear bunker—square, angular, maybe a little paunchy. He wore tailored jeans, a sport shirt, and a purple cardigan. His hair was long, swept back over his ears, and streaked with gray. He sported a Roman nose Marc Antony would envy, or at least he had until someone broke it. Now it projected, ledge-like, from his brow before plunging to the tip. His shovel chin reminded me of Basil Rathbone. His cauliflower ears told me he had been a boxer in his youth. His eyes were so brown they bordered on black. When he stared at me, it gave me the heebie-jeebies. I looked around for a cross or some holy water.

The other man I recognized from photographs. JuneBug was taller, but still topped out in the high five-feet range. His bald head gleamed, save for the fringe of artificially colored hair that ringed it. He wore the kind of thick black glasses you see in old Italian movies, the lenses tinted poker dark. He'd lost weight since the last time his picture showed up in the *Chronicle*. Like, a lot of weight. Too much. His jowls hung on either side of his chin, making him look like a malevolent ventriloquist dummy. I'm no doctor, but I didn't like his color.

Sonny gestured for me to wait. He stepped down into the main salon and spoke to JuneBug and the other man, whom I presumed to be Stan Pistone. JuneBug nodded, and Sonny crooked his finger toward me. He directed me to a chair facing the two sitting men. Seconds after I sat, the two guards from the front porch appeared on either side of me, their weapons at port arms.

"I'm flattered," I told them. "Really. But rumors of my superpowers are wildly exaggerated. I pose no danger to your bosses."

The man I presumed to be Pistone bristled at the word.

"I mean no disrespect by the term," I told him.

"So, you're Gold," JuneBug said. His voice was wheezy and sounded like he was talking through a sopping washcloth. "From what I've heard, I expected you to be eight feet tall and wearing a cape." He chuckled moistly at his own joke. Pistone chuckled. The two guys with guns chuckled. I noticed Sonny Malehala's face was grim as a headstone. "Imagine my relief to find you so…ordinary." Another round of chuckles. I had a feeling it wasn't my turn to speak, so I nodded and went along with the joke.

JuneBug turned to his partner. "Mr. Pistone. You asked for this meeting. The floor is yours."

So I was right. Stan Pistone rose to his full height. We were almost eye-to-eye. He strode across the rug separating us, and stood in front of me, his hands clasped behind his back.

"Please pardon the abrupt invitation," he said. His voice was oily, monotonous, and unequivocally uninviting. "I assure you, it wasn't without due deliberation. Sonny here confided in Mr. Bugliosi…" he gestured toward JuneBug, "…about your recent activities, and Mr. Bugliosi consulted with me. We've had several conversations regarding our response. We decided talking was the best first step. So, I would like to open with a question. Mr. Gold, where is Abner Carlisle?"

THIRTY-NINE

"Beats the hell out of me," I said. "I've met him exactly once, and it was a short conversation."

"Abner Carlisle did not hire you to find a man named Eddie Rice?" Pistone asked.

"He tried to. I refused the case."

"Why?" JuneBug wheezed.

"I wanted to avoid meetings like this, partly. Mostly, I didn't want to hitch my soul to the murder I saw in Carlisle's eyes. I sent him away."

"And yet," Pistone said. "You are still looking for Rice."

"I'm working on spec. The armored car company's insurer will pay ten percent of any portion of the heist I can recover." I didn't mention I had been hired by Jackson Pike to find Lydia Carlisle, among other things. Didn't seem relevant, and they didn't need to know everything about my work.

"How much have you recovered to date?" Pistone asked.

"Nothing."

Pistone turned to JuneBug and spread his hands. "Nothing."

"Nothing," JuneBug repeated.

"I hope to do better," I said.

"Let me ask you something," Pistone said. "It's been almost thirty years. Let's say you find Eddie Rice. Let's say he's still alive. What makes you think he still has any of the money?"

"We live in hope," I said.

"The prospects of profiting from your investment in this speculation are very poor," Pistone said.

"If I recover all of it, I can retire. I guess that's past tense now, though. Even if I did find the money, I'd have to go through you to get it to the insurance company. Right?"

"Well, it *is* our money, isn't it?" Pistone said.

"So, you have several options."

"We do," JuneBug said. It wasn't a question. He'd thought it through, too.

"I don't think you brought me here to hire me—make the search for Eddie Rice billable. You could, of course. But I don't think you did. You can make me go away. You *could* make me really, really go away, but that would get messy, and Inspector Gaddy knows I'm meeting with you tonight, so..."

"What would entice you to go away, Mr. Gold?" JuneBug said.

"Hell," I said. "I'm ninety percent there already, getting dragged across the bay by The Rock over there, to meet with men whom—and no offense intended here—I have taken great pains not to cross or interfere with. I figured out this case was a dry hole a day or so ago. Only thing driving me now is curiosity. What became of Eddie Rice and Lydia Carlisle? Where did they go? Where did the *money* go? Inquiring minds want to know. You, on the other hand, have a bigger problem."

"What is that?" JuneBug said.

"Abner Carlisle is out there. According to Inspector Gaddy, Carlisle probably already killed one of your employees, Louis Canizzaro. Carlisle might not be able to find Eddie Rice, but he knows where to find the people who financed the heist, paid off Officer Petter, and whom he might think owe him his cut."

"Nobody in his right mind would approach either myself or Mr. Bugliosi with that sort of demand," Pistone said.

"Carlisle has been in a box for twenty-three hours a day through four presidents. That much time with nothing but your thoughts will make you a little coo-coo," I said. "See, here's the problem. Carlisle's looking for you and Eddie Rice. The cops are looking for Carlisle, and they already know Canizzaro worked for you. They also know Carlisle is trying to find Rice. I'm surprised they hasn't been by to visit yet."

JuneBug waved his hand around. "Can't find us. I don't need a police inspector poking around right now. Mr. Pistone and I are on vacation. The Canizzaro thing will blow over in a week or so. Detectives move on to other things. Cases go cold."

"But you'll keep looking for Carlisle," I said.

"Naturally. There is a debt to be paid."

"No skin off my nose. There's another problem. I've been looking for Eddie Rice, but Gaddy now knows you're somehow interested in that, enough to waylay me across the bay. He's going to put two and two together and figure out this all goes back to the armored car heist. It's worth my license not to tell Gaddy what I know. Unless…"

"Yes?" JuneBug said.

"You buy what's in my head. I write the report of my search for Eddie Rice, submit it to you, you pay me for it, and my confidentiality requirements mean I keep my mouth shut. You don't waste time reinventing the wheel. Start up where I left off, and I walk away."

"You'd do that?"

"You said it. It's the only way I'm going to see anything for my efforts. I get paid for failed missing person investigations all the time. I should tell you, though, this isn't like the sanctity of the confessional. I have the right to keep whatever I tell you between us, until the second a judge tells me to spill."

"So, it's best we stay away from judges," Pistone said. "How much do you believe your information is worth?"

I told him.

"That..." he said. "That's...not much."

"I'm not a greedy man, and we're likely to get off to a better start if one of us doesn't behave like he has the other over a barrel. It's a reasonable estimate of the number of hours I've put in looking for Rice, times my hourly rate, plus expenses. You want to tip, it's up to you. I also could use the answers to a couple of questions."

"More curiosity?" JuneBug asked.

"Perhaps a little more than that. After Eddie Rice disappeared, his mother was visited by some men, regularly for a while. They always asked her whether she had heard from Eddie. Were they yours?"

JuneBug shrugged. "Hell, Gold. I don't know. Maybe. I'm not the kind of man to harass innocent family members, but in my youth, sometimes, I was in an irritable mood. I get angry. I say things. I have no memory of sending men to talk with Mrs. Rice, but it would not surprise me to discover I did. It's been thirty fucking years. Who remembers every order?"

"Just saying," I said. "If it wasn't you, and it wasn't the cops, who was it? You may have another player you don't know about."

"Some questions must necessarily go unanswered," Pistone said. "Write your report, Mr. Gold. We'll meet your terms and sign any confidentiality papers you present. Then, I believe, we shall both be thankful to be done with one another."

———————

Sonny handed my phone to me as we hopped back into the car.

"Pretty smooth in there," he said, as he dropped into gear and pulled out the driveway.

"When you're on hot coals you dance as fast as you can."

"I'd rather have your luck than a license to fucking steal."

I didn't say anything else until we were almost to Muir Woods and the bridge. "What's eating up your boss?"

Sunny scowled. "Who says anything's eating him up?"

"He's a bag of bones. His color's bad. I could see the indentations of the oxygen cannula on his cheeks. The man is sick."

We drove onto the bridge. The city ahead was remarkably fog-free. Lights twinkled in the distance.

"You meant what you said?" Sonny asked. "About showing me the ropes in your business?"

"Can't hang out a shingle until you've served time under supervision in an established PI firm," I said. "Couldn't pay you anything outside what you bill, and I'd take a cut of that for the hassle of training you. But, yeah. Sure. We could work something out. Year or so from now, you could have your own shop."

Sonny didn't speak again until we were back on dry land, in sight of the Presidio.

"JuneBug's sick," he said. "Got, like, cancer of the everything. Not going to be around much longer. Don't expect he'll see Christmas."

"That's a shame," I said. "Sucks to miss Christmas."

FORTY

I wrote the report. The money was delivered. My bank account was happy. I was not.

"You're quiet," Heidi said over dinner.

"Trying to rationalize a decision," I said. "I've sold out before. I'll do it again. It's part of the business. I don't have to like it."

"It's not exactly selling out," Heidi said. "You already admitted you probably weren't going to find the money or Rice. You had no more use for the information, so you sold it to someone who did. Sounds very American to me. I mean, if you actually had a shot at solving a twenty-five year old disappearance, and you took the money to drop the investigation, then you might be selling out. You were done, though."

My knife slipped through the steak on my plate like a scalpel opening a surgery patient. The ribeye was tender and succulent and tasty and completely wasted on me.

"I was done. I'll meet with Jackson Pike tomorrow, let him know I got about as far finding Lydia as the last guy in Sacramento. Between the hours I'll bill him, and the payment for the Eddie Rice report, I'm set for the year. Maybe we could take a trip."

"Santa Catalina?"

"Farther. I'm thinking sandy beaches, fruity drinks, warm sun, and tropical jungles. Give this leg a decent rest, let it heal. Ever been to Hawaii?"

"Never. It sounds wonderful."

"We could find out."

"I have a private show week after next. Can't get out of it. After that, I'm good until first of the year. We could do Christmas there."

"Santa surfing in a Speedo." I didn't need to say that we could do Christmas anywhere, because neither of us had any family to disappoint by showing up. "I'll check out flights and hotels tomorrow, after I talk to Pike."

———————

Inspector Gaddy and his partner Durante dropped by as I was cruising Hawaiian vacation sites on my office computer the next morning. I might have called them earlier, but I was disappointed to discover Gaddy hadn't even parked a uniform cruiser outside my building after my phone message, so I decided to let him stew and come to me.

Both Gaddy and Durante sat across from me.

"So, that was some message you sent yesterday," Gaddy said.

"It served its purpose."

"Saving your skin?"

"Among other things. You know I've been looking for Eddie Rice," I said.

"Sure. Find him yet?" Gaddy asked.

"Not looking anymore. Trail's too cold. Other people still want to talk to him, so I sold them all my information. They own it now."

"JuneBug?" Gaddy said.

I shook my head. "Confidentiality. You know me, Steve. I'm on the up and up. I found absolutely nothing in my investigation that the police need to know. I didn't find anything that would help you locate Abner Carlisle. Now that someone else owns that information, I really can't talk about it."

"You said Pistone wanted to talk to you about Carlisle."

"Sure, he asked me if I knew where Carlisle was, but I told him the truth. I haven't seen Carlisle since he stormed out of my office that one time. Yeah, I think Pistone is looking for him too. Logical assumption, since the dead guy in Carlisle's room worked for Pistone."

"What's the connection between Carlisle and Pistone? Why was Canizzaro in Carlisle's room?"

"Didn't ask, but I do have two possibilities," I said. "One, Pistone sent him to poke Carlisle for information on Eddie Rice. He poked too hard and Carlisle killed him. Second option, Carlisle was looking for Stan Pistone, found Canizzaro, and interrogated him a hair too roughly. I have a contact in Sausalito who told me JuneBug financed the armored car robbery. Like I told Pistone, he and Carlisle may be looking for each other, for different reasons. Pistone wants a piece of Carlisle's hide. Carlisle just wants to get paid. Until Canizzaro was killed, Pistone was only interested in finding Eddie Rice."

"And the money," Gaddy said.

"Mostly the money, but I think he may also be looking forward to messing Rice up a little before tossing him out a helicopter into the blades of another helicopter. Something else you should know."

"What's that?"

"Carlisle may have another reason for wanting Eddie Rice. I told you Rice ran off with Carlisle's daughter, Lydia."

"Sure."

"One of her friends told me Lydia's relationship with her father was abusive."

"Physically?" Gaddy asked.

"And sexually. A hit and kiss situation. Icky stuff. The more I hear about Carlisle, the less I like him. He presents himself as victimized, like most psychopaths. Nothing's ever his fault. Lydia was no slouch in the psychopathology department herself, but it appears she came by it honestly. Carlisle wants a chunk of Eddie Rice, because he thinks Rice stole his lover. One more thing that won't lead you to Carlisle. The cop killed in the robbery. Petter? He was dirty."

"Yeah. I know," Gaddy said. "It was in the files. IAD was already looking at him when he died. Sacramento PD swept it under the rug. Gave the rat a cop's funeral, full honors. More than one IAD officer has pissed on Petter's headstone over the years. They hate it when a bad one gets away."

"Well," I said. "He did die."

"Death Before Dishonor," Gaddy said. "So, if we want to know any more about Eddie Rice, we have to go to JuneBug."

"Sorry. He owns it now. I told him you could get a court order, but otherwise I have to maintain his privacy."

"Can never figure you out," Gaddy said, standing to leave. "Good guy or so-so guy?"

"I'm just a guy trying to make a living," I said. "Believe me, if I thought anything I have on Rice would help you find Carlisle, I'd have found a way to tell you."

FORTY-ONE

A week went by. Being bucks up for the remainder of the year gave me time to relax at the Montara house and work on the hurdy-gurdy. Having more moving parts than any other stringed instrument, there was a lot of close-in detail work to complete—chip carving, whittling a reasonable facsimile of a German headstock, building twenty or so ebony fretting keys for the melody strings. I did as much work as I could without using the power tools, just because it was quieter and more satisfying. After she closed the gallery each evening, Heidi drove down the coast to join me, which was also satisfying.

I set up my midi lathe in the carport to turn the tone wheel and the crank handle. I could have done it in my inside shop, but lathes throw shit all over the place, and it's easier to clean up outside. I was making the parts from ash, for durability. There was something deeply edifying about putting a razor-sharp gouge to the spinning blank in the lathe until ribbons of paper-thin wood shavings spew from it like the wake of a speedboat or smoke in a wind tunnel. The sound is more a low rumble than the roar of induction motors on saws and planers, accented by the hiss of the blade shaving through the grain. The hypnotic sound helped me focus and drop into a state of flow. After a while, there was nothing but me, the spinning blank, and the whisper of the skew chisel on wood.

The circular tone wheel had to have a polished surface for the rosin, so I turned it down to within a thousandth or so of its finished diameter, and cut the rest using ever-finer squares of Micromesh pressed gently against the wood as it spun. After a while, it looked is if I was polishing the polish, but I knew there were still jagged microscopic peaks in the surface of the wheel that needed to be topped and smoothed. The very last piece I put to the wood felt no more abrasive than a pad of felt. When I flipped the switch to stop the lathe, I could see my reflection in the playing surface of the wheel. Later, after removing it from the lathe mandrel, I'd chip-carve a floral design on the flat surfaces of the wheel before finishing it with stain and lacquer.

My phone vibrated in the pocket of my overalls. I ignored it. Like JuneBug and Stan Pistone, I was on vacation.

I chucked the ash blank for the hurdy-gurdy crank handle into a mandrel and suspended it between the live end and the tailstock of the lathe.

My phone vibrated again. I let it go to voicemail.

The crank handle was only four inches long, so I pulled out my pen-turning gouges and chisels, with which I could work with much greater precision. Only the last two and half inches of the handle was of a mildly mandatory barrel shape. The very end and the first inch and a half were left entirely to the creativity of the woodturner. I turned the stock into cylinder, and then marked out a series of narrow beads and coves on the spinning dowel with a mechanical pencil.

I lowered my face shield—blind detectives only find bad guys on television—and leaned a skew chisel in toward the first bead, when my phone vibrated again.

Someone was working hard to harsh my chill. I yanked off the face shield and gloves, dug the phone from my overalls pocket, and thumbed through the calls.

Steve Gaddy. Steve Gaddy. Steve Gaddy. I sighed and started to stow the phone back in my pocket, but it vibrated again. Steve Gaddy.

"This better be someone with good news or money," I said.

"JuneBug's dead," Gaddy said.

"Cancer finally got him?"

"I dunno. Does cancer come in thirty-eight caliber?"

I sat on the brick knee wall of my carport and rubbed at my face. I hadn't shaved in a week. My cheeks felt leathery and wiry. I could smell the ocean across the PCH. I wished I could throw my phone that far.

"Surprised you didn't see it on television," Gaddy said.

"Been living mostly off the grid the last week. I'm at the Montara house. What happened?"

"JuneBug arrived at his house in Pacific Heights about midnight. The place was extra quiet, because the two chuckleheads he kept for security were bleeding out from their ears in the shrubbery behind the pool. Soon as JuneBug got out of the car, someone opened fire. Got him and his bodyguard."

"Sonny Malehala?" I said.

"The guy who took you to meet with JuneBug?"

"Same guy. Ex-Ranger. A mostly good guy who keeps bad company. He was thinking about leaving JuneBug and getting into the PI business."

"He can forget about a reference letter. JuneBug was dead before he slumped to the ground."

"Malehala survived?"

"He's shot up pretty bad, but he was wearing a vest. Broke half his ribs, and he has a couple of flesh wounds, but he'll probably be out of the hospital tonight or tomorrow. We've been trying to get up with Stan Pistone but can't locate him."

"You like him for this?"

"He benefits the most."

"Doesn't sound right. JuneBug was circling the drain already. Sonny told me he had weeks at best. Pistone didn't need to splatter him. All he had to do was wait him out. I suppose you haven't found Abner Carlisle yet."

"He's on our list of probables. You know how this works, Eamon. We go after the highest probability suspect first. Since this is obviously gang shit of some sort, that's Pistone."

"Where's Sonny now?"

"Saint Francis. It was closest."

"Is he under police guard?"

"What do you think? San Francisco mob boss gets zagged, and his faithful chauffeur Kato escapes with only a few dings and scratches? Yeah. We want to keep an eye on Malehala."

"Can you tell them to let me in for a visit?" I asked.

"I'd almost insist on it. The guy's decided he doesn't like talking to cops. I know you have a history with him, so I thought maybe you'd like to drop by and pass some time."

"What happens after he gets out of the hospital?"

"We'll have questions. He may find the accommodations less cushy than a hospital room. You can save him some discomfort. Just get him to tell you who shot JuneBug, and he can sleep in his own bed tonight."

FORTY-TWO

It was my second hospital visit in less than a month. At least, this time, I wasn't the patient.

I showed my license to the cop sitting outside Sonny Malehala's hospital room. He checked a list on his clipboard and nodded me in after a quick pat down.

Sonny sat up in bed, sipping a ginger ale and watching a rugby match on television. His right bicep was wrapped in gauze and tape.

"Through and through, both rounds," he said, as I stood at the foot of the bed. "The vest caught everything else. The cops send you in here?"

"Yep," I said, watching the ruggers systematically disassemble one another on the screen. "Said you've clammed up on them."

"And they think I'll talk to *you?*"

"It seems to be their plan."

Sonny sighed. "At least you're up front about it."

"Couldn't think of a good reason for subterfuge. Does it hurt?" I pointed toward the gauze.

"Not so much right now. Good drugs. Barely touches the ribs, though. Four broken, two cracked. Fucker really lit me up. Every breath is kind of a chore. Thanks for asking."

"I've taken a round or two in the vest before. If it's any consolation, this is gonna hurt for a long, long time."

"Fuck you, Gold."

"Oh," I said. "So now you want to make up."

That did it. He cracked a smile. His chest heaved once or twice in what might have been the beginning of a laugh but ended with a grimace. "Dammit, knock it off. Hurts like hell."

"So spill, or I shall amuse you again." I collapsed into the visitor chair next to his bed.

He stared out the window, not so much for the view but because it was the opposite direction from me.

"Who do I think I'm protecting, anyway?" he said. "Trying to be a stand-up guy, so maybe Stan Pistone will be impressed, keep me on. Still interested in teaching me the private eye ropes?"

"Banged up like you are? Hell, no. Guy who can't take five or six rounds in the breadbasket without lying around in a hospital bed has no place in the business."

"Tell you what." He pointed toward my cane. "I'll be your feet on the ground if you'll be my right hand man."

He grimaced again as he almost laughed at his own joke. I chuckled, because it was kind of clever.

"You do the heavy lifting. I'll crack the jokes. Was it Carlisle?" I asked.

"Carlisle look like an albino ghost?"

"I would describe him as semi-transparent. Sure."

"That's the guy, then. Looked like the Invisible Man not quite completely reappeared. I was helping Mr. Bugliosi out of the car when he opened fire. We never had a chance. Bugliosi took a couple in the chest before I could get in front

227

of him, and I took the rest of that magazine in the back. Soon as it stopped, I started to drag him around the car, but Carlisle opened up again. I dove to the ground, shielding Bugliosi, but two rounds got through, went through my arm, and finished him off. That's when I saw the shooter. He wore jeans and a black hoodie, but the hood was down and I saw his face and hands. Fucker is so white, he fuckin' glows in the dark."

"Did he say anything?"

"Yeah, Gold. He said *bang bang bang* a whole bunch of fuckin' times, and it was really, really loud. For all I know, he was singing fuckin' show tunes. After the first couple of shots, I couldn't hear shit. Just the ringing in my ears. Still ringing. Does that shit ever go away?"

"Nah. You learn to live with it."

"Fuck. Someone said they have a cop outside the door."

"Uniform kid. Seems nice. Green. Not the kind of officer they'd assign if they expect a mob invasion. I think he's more intended to keep you inside than to keep anyone else out. In your weakened state, he might even pull it off."

"The cops think I had something to do with Mr. Bugliosi's murder?"

"I think they're focused more on Stan Pistone. More to gain. Any chance Pistone might want you to carry the weight for JuneBug? Knock it off with the threatening glare. The guy was a murdering psychopath in his day, and now he's a dead psychopath and won't be signing any more paychecks. He is who he was. Don't look at me that way."

"I don't think Pistone is a problem for me," Sonny said, after some thought. "Nothing to gain. I don't think Carlisle is a threat to me. No motive. Jesus, Gold. You know what I was?"

"No, Sonny. What were you?" I asked.

"The innocent bystander," he said. "I was fuckin' collateral damage."

FORTY-THREE

Apparently, Steve Gaddy and Jasper Durante shared Sonny's
assessment of his status as collateral damage, because Gaddy
pulled the police watch from Sonny's room a few hours later.
When I told them Sonny had identified Abner Carlisle as
JuneBug's killer, Steve was stoic, but I could hear the
disappointment in his voice. He wanted to make his bones
putting gangsters away, not chasing people who might be
performing a public service by offing them. Steve's a good
cop and a hell of a nice guy, but not a terribly abstract
thinker. Moral dilemmas put him in a tizzy.

I sat in my car outside the patient release at St. Francis
Hospital the next morning and watched as a kid in green
orderly scrubs wheeled Sonny Malehala through the
automatic doors. I pulled my car to the curb in front of them.

"Gold?" Sonny asked, as I opened the passenger side
door. "You're picking me up?"

"Why not?" I said. "You already have a ride?"

"Figured I'd just call a cab," Sonny said.

"Save you the taxi fare. Hop in."

The kid turned the wheelchair around after Sonny
gingerly twisted himself into the passenger seat. When I slid
behind the wheel, I realized he took up his half of the car,
and not a small percentage of mine.

"What in hell do you bench, anyway?" I asked as I pulled away from the curb. He told me. I was duly impressed and said so. "Well, those days are over, Lefty. You're gonna need rehab on that shot-up arm of yours, and it's going to be months before those ribs can support much more than your own weight. What kind of Workman's Comp situation does the mob sport, anyway?"

"I get it," he said. "I'm fucked."

"As gangland muscle, I'd say your short but eventful career was a bust. You seem smart, though. Ninety percent of the work I do is research, talking to people without scaring them to death, and sitting in cars waiting for something to happen, and the rest is writing reports. I figure, while you're recuperating, I can show you the ropes. No salary, but you can keep what you bill. You might hit a bit of a snag when it comes to licensing because of your recent employment, but while you're training, we'll cultivate some impressive legitimate references."

"I asked you before why you'd do something like that for me. You brushed it off."

"I've been lucky lately," I said. "Just paying it forward. Where are we headed?"

He told me. A pricey address. Sonny Malehala had done very nicely working for JuneBug.

"You know how to get there?" he asked.

"Oh, yeah," I said. "And you are gonna have to bill a buttload of hours."

Sonny assured me that he had substantial savings from his years guarding JuneBug and wouldn't be in dire straits for some time. I thought that sounded like a delightful condition to be in, and I said so. Then I realized I was in a substantially similar situation myself and figured we both could benefit from some rest and rehab.

"It's going to be six weeks at least before you can laugh comfortably," I told him. "Kick back until the first of the year and give me a call. I think Heidi and I are spending the holidays in Hawaii anyway."

"Heidi?"

"You'll see. Can't miss her. Force of nature."

I dropped him off at his home and pointed the car back toward Montara.

Once there, I changed into my overalls and a sweatshirt. Thick, frying-pan clouds hung in the air just offshore, and I could see telltale curtains of water falling on the horizon. In hours, we'd be socked in.

As rain began to pock at the windows, I shaped the top bracing of the hurdy-gurdy using razor-sharp chisels and scrapers, made the final fitting and installation of the crank and wheel, and closed up the soundbox for good with a healthy bead of aliphatic resin glue and dozens of violin clamps I'd cobbled together from ash dowels, felt, butterfly nuts, and eight inch carriage bolts. Building the soundbox was the easiest part. It was only slightly different than any of several dozen guitar soundboxes I'd built over the years, the primary divergence being heavier bracing to support the crank assembly. Otherwise, it was Lutherie 101.

Now came the hard part. While it appeared an impossibly Byzantine instrument, the hurdy-gurdy only had two primary parts—the soundbox with its crank and wheel; and a heavy keybox that floated on the spruce top of the soundbox. The keybox would be constructed of the same claro walnut as the soundbox and would contain two dozen hand carved ebony keys. The keys tuned any or all of the three melody strings that coursed through the keybox to play melodies or chords.

I had already marked the sides of the keybox at the correct positions for the keyholes and would carve each one by hand after hogging out the centers on the drill press. I'd also rough sawn the ebony keys themselves and looked forward to shaping and smoothing them to their final dimensions with rasps and scrapers. It would be nice to finish the hurdy-gurdy before winging off to the tropical Land of Weeky-Wacky, but if I didn't, I decided it didn't matter much. The guy I was building it for didn't have me on a deadline. If I didn't finish before we left, I'd do it when we get back. Better to do it right than do it fast. I put the work aside and headed to the kitchen for a beer, reflexively repeating a saying my dad drilled into me. "Nobody ever seems to have time to do it right, but everyone finds time to do it over."

I had started to walk short distances without my cane, but still found it tiring and achy. It might still be a week or so before I'd be able to walk to the corner and back without aid. I'd already resigned to taking it to Hawaii, though. I hoped to need it less and less over the course of the trip.

For now, I needed it for a trip longer than ten feet or so, which included a dash to the fridge. I reached for the door handle just as my phone buzzed. I really didn't want to talk with Steve Gaddy again. He'd been nothing but Bad News Bobby for days.

It wasn't Gaddy. The screen read *B. Ledford.*

"Barbara," I said.

"Eamon. I'm so sorry it took so long to get those age progression renderings to you. Things got busy. We're getting scoped out by some new outfit in Silicon Valley. No details available yet, but it looks good. I might retire soon."

"Good news," I said. I had almost forgotten about Eddie Rice's junior high photo. When I sold all my information to Pistone, I sort of back-burnered the case to concentrate on woodworking and vacation planning. I couldn't recall whether I'd included Barbara's name in the stuff I handed over to Pistone. In any case, with JuneBug dead, Pistone was probably too busy transitioning to his new role in the Bugliosi organization, in whatever form it might take, to keep pursuing a ghost. "Were you able to get anything usable from the school picture?"

"Oh, Eamon, baby, were we! I owe you a ton. I mentioned my colleague? The cute kid with the image-sharpening software and the MILF fetish?"

"I recall."

"Interesting coincidence. Seems our separate programs potentiate one another."

"Those naughty little devils."

"When we filtered the picture you gave me through his system and then through mine, somehow the aging filters provided greater definition to the rasterized fillers, resulting in a level of resolution almost equal to..."

"Time out," I said. "Dumb person version."

"You know how age-progression pictures sometimes look a lot like those facial reconstructions done on skulls?"

"Sure."

"Not very lifelike. What we have looks like we took a photo of the guy yesterday. In high-definition. Eight-fuckin'-K baby!" She let out a brief victory whoop over the phone.

"You screwed the kid, didn't you?" I said.

"Had to fuckin' celebrate, Eamon! Been a while since I bounced around with a guy in his twenties. They know more these days."

"All that Internet porn."

"Bless their little hearts. Where do they get the energy? So, yeah, I banged the little cutie. Gonna do it again. And, we are going to be *rich*. I owe it partly to you. If you hadn't brought in that crappy yearbook photo, I wouldn't have consulted with Benny, and we wouldn't know how compatible our programs were. We are going to fucking *own* the milk carton franchise."

"You want to squirt one percent my way, I won't argue," I said.

"We'll mention you in the patent."

"Even better. So, what does Eddie Rice look like today?" I asked.

I heard computer keys tapping on the other end of the line. Then Barbara said, "I'm sending you four renderings. All of them project the image you gave me to approximately age seventy. To account for variables about which we have no data—male pattern baldness, facial hair, that sort of thing—I've sent you two progressions with baldness and two with hair. I also projected a mustache on each of the two hair types. I can tell you, since Benny and I discovered how our programs work together, we've run comparisons on four or five other child pictures for whom we have adult counterparts. The resemblance was startling. We really

235

Richard Helms

stumbled on something here. Pair this with facial recognition software tied into massive CCD camera systems such as those in London, and you can find missing people in minutes."

"You're busting my balls, Babs," I said. "You know finding people puts groceries on my table. I want that one percent now."

"Maybe a stock deal? I'm telling you; we have discovered something incredible here."

As she spoke, I booted my laptop and accessed my email. Seconds later, the screen populated with four images. I scrolled down until the third one made my hand freeze on the mouse.

"I think you have," I said. "In fact, I know where to find this man. You hit a home run your first step up to the plate, Barbara. Remember me in your will."

"That I can do!" she said. "I'd better do it quickly, though, because another night with Benny might put me in a hospital."

Five hours later, I was in Mill Valley. I walked up to the front porch of the Pike house and banged on the door.

Jackson Pike answered several seconds later. Despite the hour, he was still dressed in jeans and a sport shirt. Gray chest hairs poked out above the vee neck of the shirt. He held an Anchor Steam beer in his hand.

"How's it hangin', Eddie?" I asked.

FORTY-FOUR

Jackson Pike—or Eddie Rice—had a couple of choices. If he had been carrying a gun when he answered the door, he could have shot me, buried me in the backyard, and ditched my car.

He didn't have a gun, of course. Why would he? He didn't even know I was coming. That left him with Option B, which was to ask me into the house and try to lie his way out of it.

"Get you a beer?" he asked.

"Sure."

I followed him into the kitchen, to make sure he wasn't dashing for some artillery. He knew what I was doing, but he didn't fight me over it.

"I wasn't expecting you, Gold. When the bell rang, I thought it was Gene Haake. He's supposed to drop by this evening with some plans for a new strip mall. Joan's still out of town," he said.

"Probably better that way."

He reached into the fridge and handed me a Steam and a church key. I popped the cap and placed the opener back on the counter.

"Let's go to my office," he suggested.

He sat at his desk

I stood next to the display case.

"What gave me away?" he asked.

I tapped the picture of him driving a stock car in Canada. "The pieces fell together. You were a racer. Eddie Rice was the wheelman for the heist. I ran histories on Abner Carlisle, on Lydia, hell, even on Joan. I ran them on all your employees. The only person I didn't check was you. After all, you were the client. Why would I peek into your past? Imagine my surprise when I discovered you apparently materialized from the ether only twenty-five years ago. There's no record of Jackson Pike before then."

"Money can buy a lot," he said. "It can't always buy a fleshed-out past."

"I have a buddy at Berkeley who's working on a new age progression computer algorithm. I gave her Eddie Rice's junior high photo and told her to pile on forty or fifty years and add some silver and a moustache." I withdrew the printout from my jacket pocket and handed it to him. "Nice likeness."

He examined the picture. "I'm carrying less weight in my face, but there is definitely a resemblance."

"This was the kicker," I said, as I hobbled to the wall and rapped a knuckle on the race car picture. "The sponsor on the race car. *Atlas Controls*. I ran across that name on a convoluted list of shell corporations paying for Calliope Rice's retirement home."

"It was one of my first companies," he said. "Defunct, now, for all intents and purposes, except as a name on a corporate spreadsheet."

"With a periodically active bank account. By the way, your mom sends her regards. She'd like to know what became of you."

"Yes. So. You've found Eddie Rice. What now? Are you going to turn me in?"

"For what? Statute of limitations ran out on the robbery years ago. Nobody wants to hear Walt Petter's name again, so you skate on the murder charges."

"I mean to Pistone."

"I already sold you to Pistone. Sort of. He bought all my records of the search for Eddie Rice, which amounted to a big box of nothing. He doesn't have the pictures. I don't like Pistone, though. I think maybe I'm finished selling stuff to him. Fact is, I planned to meet with you today anyway, to tell you the likelihood of finding Lydia was extremely low, and maybe you were wasting your money."

"It's mine to waste."

"Maybe I don't like wasting my time. Now, though...well, I'll settle for answers. Here's the way I see it. You were working for Stan Pistone, as part of the A Team. Abner Carlisle, Ells, Podnow, Pietke, they were all the B Team. They were expendable. Their job was to be pathetically incompetent and hopefully get their asses shot off while you, Pistone, and the rest of the A Squad made off with the money. You were the lynch pin between the groups. You recruited Carlisle, made him think the heist was his idea, and let him put together his team of mental defectives."

"There are some...inaccuracies in your story," he said. "But not enough to matter."

"You didn't count on Walt Petter and his flat tire, though. When the flag went down, and the bullets started to fly, you saw an opportunity to rabbit with all that cash. Twenty extra large is a huge motivation to double-cross your buddies, and maybe back then Pistone wasn't as scary as he is today."

"You make me sound almost intelligent," he said.

"Oh, I think you're bright enough, Eddie..."

"Please," he said. "Eddie Rice died a long time ago. I'm Jack Pike."

"Bet you still carry Rice's fingerprints."

He held up his hands, palms out, and wiggled his digits.

"You want to print me, Gold?"

"Tell me about Lydia."

He drained the last of his bottle and tossed it into the trash.

"Lydia," he said, as he reached into a mini-fridge next to his desk for another. "You know how, sometimes, you see a guy tooling around town in a hot car, and you know you could drive it ten times better than he can? Lydia was dating boys. I was pushing forty. Some cars, though, nobody can drive. They fool you into thinking you can control them, and then they wheelspin on you when you least expect it. It was wild at first, a real E-Ticket ride, but after a while I realized it was... really *crowded* in her head. She was totally into sensation—pure, unfiltered sensation. There wasn't a shred of emotion in her that wasn't attached to some self-serving need. She was Daddy's girl, all the way."

"That's the way I hear he liked her."

"Yeah. That was ugly. I didn't find out about that until...well, late. Maybe Abner was so in love with his little girl, however sick and exploitative that love became, that he never saw the little monster she really was. Maybe he saw her all too well and chose to ignore what she was because she had him wrapped around her little finger. Once Abner crossed the line, Lydia could get anything she wanted from him. After he went away, she turned to any man who could give her what she wanted, and just sucked him dry before moving on."

"You ran off with her anyway."

"Before I realized how... *sick* she was. It was like watching a tragic movie unfold in front of my eyes, totally aware of how it was going to end, and knowing there was nothing I could do to stop it. She knew I had money, but I never told her how much or where it came from, because she would have run through it in a couple of weeks. It was always about raising the stakes for Lydia, and no matter how much I thought I cared for her, I couldn't get her to put on the brakes.

"We never stayed in one place two nights straight. Before we took off, I had stashed money in bus depot lockers all over the western half of the country. Whenever we ran low, I'd head for one of them, stock back up, and then we were back on the road. When there was money, we stayed in nice places. When there wasn't much, not so nice."

"She wrote letters. She never mentioned you," I said.

"Because I told her not to. I was on the run, Gold. From the fucking mob! That's the kind of stuff you only see in the movies. Hell, I was on the run from the minute I turned right instead of left in the rental van after the robbery. Soon as I missed the meetup, I was dead. I went underground. Couch-surfed until I ran out of buddies. Lived in a van for a while, which wasn't nearly as nice as it sounds. Managed to stay under JuneBug's radar, somehow, and still visit Abner in prison once or twice. That's where I tested out my fake ID's."

"Kind of a high risk place to flash around false papers."

"What can I say? I was a hyperactive thrill seeker."

"So how'd you hook up with Lydia?"

"Like I said. Couch-surfing. I'd used up my friends north of the city, but I still wanted the bay between me and JuneBug. I drifted into Berkeley and looked her up. Abner had told me she was going to school there. I finagled a chance meeting, and one thing led to another. Big mistake. Biggest mistake of my life."

"What happened to her?" I asked.

"She died in Elko, Minnesota, on a Sunday morning in February. At least I'm pretty sure it was in the morning. I woke up and found her in the bathroom, spike still stuck in her arm, froth dried on her mouth. It was hideous."

"What did you do with her?" I asked.

"What could I do? It wasn't like I could call the local funeral home and have them pick her up. I waited until Monday. I sat in vigil, with her wrapped in the motel sheet on the floor next to the bed, all day Sunday, until late that night. Then I got her into the trunk of the car and drove out to a local lake. I broke into an ice fishing house, weighted her down with chains, and dropped her through the hole. I reckon she's still there."

"What about the money?" I asked. "It was twenty million, after all. You couldn't have burned through all of it on the road."

"The money?" he asked, his eyes damp and reddened. "Hell, Gold, it's all around you. It's in this house. It's in the cars in the garage. It's in the land, the clothes on my back, the boots on my feet, in Joan's jewelry case. It's in every company I own, and a few more. After I dumped...after Lydia died, Eddie Rice ceased to exist, and Jackson Pike was born. I changed my hair. Hell, it was changing itself by then." He rubbed the bare skin on top of his head. "I grew a moustache, started working out, and I crossed the Canadian border and took a job working in the oil fields in the Northern Territories. Turns out I had a talent for it. After I learned the business, I paid cash for some spec land to sink a couple of wells. Next thing I knew, I had multiplied my armored car money several times. The money became the foundation for my business. I went straight and found out there was a lot more money in it. Go figure."

"And what about Joan? What happened there? You figured the daughter was so good in bed you'd see what it was like to boink the mother?"

His ears reddened, and he gripped the bottle so hard I expected the glass to burst.

"Cripple or not, I should crush you for that," he said.

"It's a natural question."

"You're pushing it, Gold."

"Set me straight, then."

"It was an accident. I had moved to San Francisco. I'd always liked the city, and now I could afford to live there in style. Nobody had seen Eddie Rice in over two decades, and I have one of those faces that age more quickly. Maybe it's true what they say about years and mileage. Anyway, I was hiding in plain sight, under a completely new identity, reasonably certain I was safe from JuneBug or anyone else.

"I went to this dinner party, and a woman I knew introduced me to Joan. I almost didn't recognize her. I'd only seen her before from a distance. When I realized who she was, I almost walked away clean. She represented a past I didn't want to revisit. Fate in the form of place cards at dinner threw us together anyway. We talked for a while, and she had too much to drink, and I offered to drive her home.

"She started talking about her husband in the car, and then she moved on to her missing daughter, and then she lost it. I spent most of the night holding her as she cried her eyes out over her little girl, and all I could think about was Lydia lying on the bottom of that fishing lake in Minnesota, and what she had looked like skagged out on the floor of the motel bathroom."

"So? What? You gave her a mercy marriage?"

"Maybe I felt as if I owed her. In all likelihood, she would have lost her daughter with or without me, but as it played out Joan lost Lydia because of me. When I realized how badly I had hurt her, I decided I had to make that right. Marrying her, hiring the private detective, all of it—it gave her a little hope. That hope rejuvenated her. After a few years, I realized I really liked Joan. A couple more years, and I came to love her—the real love, I mean. The kind of love that comes after you stop noticing the wrinkles and the gray roots in her hair and the inevitable sags of time and the pull of the earth."

"Now you're just being poetic."

"Something else I acquired after Lydia. As she sank to the bottom of that lake, I realized I was sick and tired of a life full of ugly. I decided right then I would learn about beautiful things, try to find some peace in my life. Anyway, I love Joan, Mr. Gold. I'd do anything to protect her from being hurt again."

"So you hired me, and then you sent me on fool's errands to get me off her back. If I did a truly meticulous search of your property, where precisely would I locate thirty feet of detcord?"

He smiled. "You might be guessing," he said.

"The guys at ATF never received a report of missing explosives from you," I said. "But they were very curious as to why I was asking."

"Okay. Another ploy. It's stowed in a storage building out back of the house, under lock and key. A really *good* lock this time. All the other stuff is there too. When you came to ask about Lydia, I figured you were just another dumb strung-out fortune seeker, or another stupid shamus like the one I'd hired just after I'd married Joan. I figured if I threw a few dollars at you, you'd go away."

"Sorry to disappoint you. With Eddie Rice back in the picture, things are complicated. I was ninety percent convinced you were dead."

"Thank you. My efforts weren't entirely wasted," he said.

"Now that you're alive, you need to answer some questions. Nobody knows yet who killed the guy in Abner Carlisle's hotel room. Everyone presumes Carlisle did it, but you have a motive as well. Maybe you heard Carlisle was out of jail and sniffing around, and you knew that if he ever laid eyes on you the game was over. Maybe you paid him a visit and killed the wrong guy."

"No," Pike said. "Like I said, I'm through with the ugly side of life. Let me show you something."

He walked out of the kitchen. For a moment, I wondered whether he was about to dash out the door and take his act on the road again. Part of me wanted to follow him. The rest of me figured it really didn't matter anymore. I'd found Eddie Rice and the money and would probably get squat for my efforts.

Oh, I suppose I could blackmail him. I've known PIs who did that sort of thing. They never did it for long. Besides, I'd already made another month's nut writing up his security plans, and the bill I'd send him for my search for Lydia was going to be a whopper. So it wasn't a complete loss. And, Heidi had lost her bet. I hadn't come up empty-handed, so she owed me fifty bucks.

And that thing I like so much.

Pike returned to the kitchen several moments later, with a leather packet folded and wrapped in a cotton ribbon. He pulled the knot on the ribbon, and the packet rolled open.

"I knew Abner would get out of prison someday. I had made some discreet inquiries over the years, and he was the only one left from the original B Team, as you call them. About five years ago, I set up a trust for him."

He passed the papers in the leather packet over to me. They were legal forms, establishing a trust account in the name of Abner Carlisle. The original investment had been six million dollars.

"His cut, plus what I figured the interest amounted to after fifteen years," Pike explained. "I knew Abner couldn't stay away from Joan for long after getting out of prison. I figured he'd show up here one day, if only to lay eyes on her.

When he did, it was a dead certainty he would recognize me. He's been obsessed with me for three decades, after all."

"You planned to give him this?"

"Joan wanted nothing to do with Carlisle. I planned to give him the money and ask him to go to Mexico or Canada with it. It was the only way I could think of to get him out of our lives."

"And what about Lydia? What did you plan to tell him about his daughter?"

"That Lydia ran off with another guy within days of running off with me, and I had lost track of her. After what he did to Lydia, I could lie to him with a straight face all day long. Even so, he spent a third of his life expectancy and a little more behind bars. I figured, even if he was a child-molesting sack of shit, he'd earned his take from the robbery."

"You had it all planned out," I said.

"I wanted to make things right, and I wanted him to go away forever."

"It's too late for that. Your trust fund is worthless to Carlisle now. He's on the run for murder. The guy got out of prison only a few weeks ago. The cops are going to treat him like a mad dog. He can't just walk into Wells Fargo and make a withdrawal. Wherever your wife is? Maybe you should go there too, until the police have him in custody."

The doorbell rang. "You might be right," Pike told me as he stood. "That's Gene Haake. I'll hustle him along, and we can talk about arrangements. I'll be right back."

I sat in the office. I heard the door open, and a familiar voice.

"Pardon me, sir. I'm looking for Joan Pike. Is this the right ad...what the *fuck?*"

Abner Carlisle had also found Eddie Rice.

FORTY-FIVE

It sounded as if Pike tried to talk, but Carlisle wasn't in the mood. I heard a crash and the rip of splitting wood, and I envisioned the pretty little cherry occasional table that had stood by the front door, now probably kindling. I stood and limped to the office door as quickly as I could and heard the wet slaps of fists on skin, and the grunts of determined men locked in fatal combat. A ceramic lamp crashed to the floor, as I tried to figure out how to intervene.

I wasn't wearing a weapon. I was hobbled by a bad leg. Pike hadn't called out to me when he saw Carlisle at the door, so maybe he thought he was protecting me. Maybe he thought he could take Carlisle without my help, but I'd met the man, and he looked as if he'd spent his twenty-three hours a day in solitary over the last twenty-five years doing pushups. From the sounds in the living room, both Carlisle and Pike were giving as much as they were taking. They were both old men, but in great shape for their ages.

Across the hall from the office was the dining room, which was connected by French doors to a solarium. The living room was directly across from the solarium, so I thought I could get closer without giving myself away.

I reached the solarium at the exact moment Gene Haake walked through the open front door. He carried a mailing tube in his hand, which fell to the floor as he saw Carlisle and Pike throwing each other off the walls and trading punches with fists now dripping blood. Each roundhouse that landed sprayed Jackson Pollack patterns on the neutral plastered walls.

"What in hell?" Haake shouted. "Mr. Pike! I'm calling the police!"

He reached for his cell phone, which I had to admit was a smarter move than I'd made so far. At least, it looked smart until Carlisle yanked a pistol from under his jacket and pointed it toward Haake.

I whirled around the corner and swung my cane down as hard as I could. Really put my weight into it. The crook smashed into Carlisle's wrist. I heard bones snap, and the pistol dropped to the floor. I pivoted and kicked the gun across the hardwood floor and under the sofa. I was just turning back to Carlisle when a train ran into the side of my head. I heard a sound like a sledgehammer striking a muted bell, and everything in my field of vision turned crimson. I didn't feel myself fall. It felt more like floating, even when I hit the floor and bounced once or twice, and I heard a distant echo of another ceramic lamp shattering, and the last thought through my head before the world winked out was, "Oh, great. Another fucking concuss…"

I was probably out for only a minute or so, because nature is a cruel bastard, and it doesn't want you to miss the blinding pain that sets in as soon as your nerve endings adjust to the shock of a fist trying to drill through your skull.

Haake shook me, repeatedly. "Mr. Gold. Are you okay?"

"No, for fuck sake," I mumbled. "I got my bell rung by Quasimodo over there."

At least, I think I said that. I might have just thought it. My memory of that part of the evening is still a little blurry. I slowly rolled onto my side and tried to sit up. Someone lit off a grenade in my head, which I found unpleasant, so I leaned back against the sofa.

Haake kept looking at my pupils for some reason. Across the room, Carlisle lay on his stomach, his arms straight at his sides, in a field of broken porcelain. He snored softly, blowing little blood and spit bubbles from the side of his mouth. Pike stood over him, his face swollen and bloody. He wrapped Carlisle's wrists behind his back with duct tape. Carlisle's feet were already bound. In the distance, I heard the wail of sirens.

"What in hell happened?" Haake demanded. "Who is that man?"

"Abner Carlisle," Pike said, as he ripped the tape and secured Carlisle's hands. "My wife's first husband. He's a felon. Just got out of prison. Apparently, he was looking for Joan. Mr. Gold had just warned me Carlisle might be headed this way, and there he was. Carlisle was upset that Joan wasn't here, and he...well, he just went crazy. Right, Gold? That's how you saw it?"

He was constructing his cover. It worked, because it was completely true, except for the reason Carlisle attacked Pike. But...details, right? I figured it was as good a story as any.

"Sure," I said. "Whatever. What'd he hit me with?"

"His fist," Haake said. "Hardest I've ever seen anyone hit. You were out like a light."

251

"You broke his wrist, though. Gave me time to hit him with the lamp," Pike said. "That put him down."

"Great. I get the assist," I slurred. For some reason, my mouth wasn't working correctly. I reached up and touched my face, only to find the entire right side twice its usual size. Haake headed down the hallway to get a first aid kit and some ice.

"Cops and an ambulance are on the way," Pike said. "There are going to be a lot of questions."

"Yup," I said. "You going with that whopper you just told?"

"It's mostly true."

"You can't keep this up," I said. "Jackson Pike had a great run, but I think it's over. Carlisle's going to out you."

"You might be right. Second time I've said that tonight."

The sirens grew closer, and I could see revolving red and blue lights in the distance through the trees.

"Keep a secret?" he said.

"It's kind of my thing," I said.

"Joan knows everything. Has for years. It was incredibly tough. Came within seconds of ending our marriage. We rebuilt, though. I had a plan for Carlisle here..." He patted the snoring man on the back. "I have a plan for us. Jack and Joan Pike are going to have an unfortunate accident—the kind that doesn't leave a lot of evidence behind. I have money squirreled away all over the world, Gold. I have go bags with different new IDs for both of us in dozens of safe deposit boxes. Eddie Rice earned a doctorate in disappearing. He's been on the run, always looking over his shoulder, for thirty years. Do anything that long, and you become an expert. Joan isn't visiting relatives. She's in a house we own under another identity, in another city, in another country, waiting for me to set up our…departure. That's why I sent you on fools' errands. I was buying time to make our arrangements. As soon as you knocked on our door, we knew it was time. That's why she was so upset when you showed up. See, Gold? I always had an escape strategy. By the time anyone listens to Carlisle's ravings about Eddie Rice, Jack and Joan Pike will be nothing more than tragic memories. There's only one problem."

"I could still sell you out," I said.

"Yeah. I don't think you will, though."

I rubbed my aching cheek. "Why?"

"You didn't run to Pistone the minute you figured out who I was. You came to me. Maybe you don't even know why. But I recognize loyalty when I see it."

"Maybe I'm into closure. Maybe I wanted to see you twist a little before I dropped the noose around your neck."

"Not you. What will it take, Gold? Give me a little more time? For Joan? I can set you up for life, if you want."

Emergency vehicles parked in front of the house, their lights bouncing around the room, the sirens dying as cops and medical workers jumped from their cars and headed toward the front door.

"I'll bill you for my time looking for Lydia, and my expenses. I did the work and deserve to be paid."

"That's it?" he asked.

"You want to toss in a tip, that's between you and your conscience."

FORTY-SIX

The bruise that had formerly been the right side of my face did not go away completely before Heidi and I boarded our cruise ship for Honolulu. Between my purple and yellow mottled features and my renewed need for my cane, I drew more than my share of stares at the bar.

Every time I noticed someone zeroed in on me, I'd turn to Heidi and say, loudly enough to be heard two decks down, "So there I was. Forty thousand feet. Engine flamed out. The fighter jet was in a flat spin and dropping like a stone. I had two choices. Wrestle the nose down and try to force enough air through the engines to reignite; or punch out. I waited until I passed ten thousand feet, then I reached for the ejection trigger handles, said a quick Hail Mary, and blew myself into the sky."

People looked at me differently after that. Looks of pity turned to awe. I saw one woman at dinner pointing at me and whispering to her friend. I figured I had gone too far when some guy wearing a VFW cap bought me a drink and thanked me for my service. After that, I kept things on the DL. I'm a straight arrow, but I can still tell a whopper when it suits me.

Before we left, Steve Gaddy filled me in on some of the details I missed. Once in custody, Carlisle did try to claim

Pike was Eddie Rice, but nobody listened because they were much more interested in how Louis Canizzaro wound up dead in Carlisle's room, and what possible connection that might have to the abattoir police found at Stan Pistone's compound in Pacifica. According to Gaddy, Carlisle remembered Canizzaro and tracked the man down in a bar. There, he plied the man with drinks, enough to make Canizzaro only marginally conscious. Back at the hotel room, Carlisle extracted Pistone's location from Canizzaro before dispatching him.

Before Carlisle killed him, Pistone told Carlisle he had been looking for Eddie Rice, and had a juicy lead. I had mentioned Jackson Pike in my notes, but only in passing as the husband of Joan Carlisle, and Pistone handed that report to Carlisle, bargaining for his life. That's what led Carlisle to Mill Valley. For his efforts, Pistone had his head crushed. Gaddy described the crime scene as a vomit party.

So Carlisle was going down for the murders of JuneBug, Canizzaro, and Pistone. When he realized he had left prison after nearly three decades only to go right back in, he went a little crazy.

Crazier, that is.

He assaulted the guards escorting him to his cell, then picked fights with enough guys in gen pop at the jail to earn some alone time. Deep down, I think that's what he really wanted. It was probably the closest thing to home he could recall. Because he appeared so out of control, nobody was interested in his ravings about Eddie Rice, the last armored car robber. They saw it as just one more piece of his unending paranoid gibberish. I thought Carlisle might be crazy like a fox. An insanity plea only works once in a hundred times it's tried, but Carlisle might just pull it off and spend the rest of his life in a cushy mental hospital.

I kept my promise and called John Rascoe at the insurance company as soon as I returned to my office a day or so after being released from the hospital. He already knew about Carlisle's arrest, because of course he did. The robbery was his hobby.

I told him I'd located Eddie Rice, which delighted him. He listened raptly as I detailed Eddie's fugitive run across the country. He seemed legitimately upset when he heard Lydia's fate. I didn't tell him where Eddie dumped the body, and I didn't give away Eddie's new identity. I was still deciding where my loyalties lay. I finally decided I delayed because I liked Jack Pike, when all is said and done, and I wanted to see if he'd make good on his promise to disappear. Rascoe is a smart man, though. He's probably figured it out already. Not that it matters much.

Right before I left, I received a call from Mr. Ellroy, the director at Shady Oaks Retirement Home. He told me two people had visited Calliope Rice the night before. He described Jack and Joan Pike perfectly. Afterward, Calliope couldn't stop talking about her visitors with the facility staff. She told one of them she had seen her son for the first time in decades. Ellroy asked me whether they might be trouble. I told him not to worry. He would probably never see them again.

We had satellite TV in our stateroom during the crossing to Honolulu. For several days, the lead story on the news was the ongoing search for a missing airplane piloted by wealthy Mill Valley oil man and land developer Jackson Pike and his wife Joan. The airplane had disappeared from air traffic radar while offshore, flying north toward Vancouver. The rate of descent was consistent with sudden and extreme airframe failure—the kind that might result from the detonation of thirty feet of detcord, for instance. Searchers were optimistic, but I knew better. The Pikes were destined to join the ranks of Judge Crater, D.B. Cooper, and Jimmy Hoffa.

I remembered the picture of Jack and Joan in Pike's office, in which they celebrated a successful skydiving jump. I knew they were happily slipping into new lives in faraway places with strange sounding names, but I kept that to myself. Pike was my client, after all. He wasn't the first criminal who'd hired me. He was, however, by far the most successful one. Also, it turns out Jackson Pike is a heavy tipper. I like to encourage that sort of behavior.

Heidi and I lounged on Waikiki Beach, which was remarkably more crowded than I had anticipated. Since I was bucks-up, I splurged on a cabana which came with food and beverage service. Diamond Head rose to our left. It was Christmas Eve, and a balmy eighty degrees, the tradewinds rustling the canvas of our cabana and cooling the condensation on our mai-tai glasses. Over the last week, I had become quite the mai-tai connoisseur.

Heidi had doffed her silk beach robe, revealing a banana-yellow bikini that was little more than spaghetti straps and butt floss. All the better to apply sunscreen, I reasoned, because I spend a lot my time rationalizing my lustful thoughts about Heidi, and—being quintessentially northern European—she uses a *lot* of sunscreen.

In the end, she'd insisted on splitting the cost of the trip, so we were giving it to each other as our Christmas presents. Later that evening, we had dinner rezzies at the revolving restaurant Top of Waikiki, after which we'd find a way to stay awake long enough for Santa to get to Hawaii.

"Thank you," she said, lazily, as waves lapped against the sugar sands. A lone surfer waded into the water, carrying his board at this side. He dropped the board, pushed it past the breaker waves, and then climbed on to paddle out.

"For what?"

"The trip. Not getting killed. Stuff like that."

"My pleasure. You know, I'm not a complete idiot."

"There's room for improvement?" she asked.

"I know we said the trip was our big present to one another. I'm not about to get caught empty handed tomorrow morning, though. There's something small and sparkly, back in the room," I said.

"Sounds lovely. I got you something, too. You like socks, right?"

"You still owe me for our bet. You said I'd never find Eddie Rice. I found him."

"Oh, yeah. Almost forgot. I owe you that thing you like so much. Right?"

"Not to be pushy."

She watched as the surfer paddled furiously to catch a wave timed to break just past him. He rolled the nose of the board over the crest and rose to his feet.

"Won't do eight seconds," she said. "Double or nothing."

The kid was lean and lanky and sun-bronzed, with long peroxide hair and a dumb soul patch under his lower lip. He looked like he surfed a lot. Might have been a local, weaned on coconut milk after being born on a surfboard in the back of a woody to Gidget and Moondoggie. He looked calm and confident.

"You're on," I said.

I love a sure thing.

ABOUT THE AUTHOR

Richard Helms is a retired forensic psychologist and college professor. He has been nominated eight times for the SMFS Derringer Award, winning it twice; six times for the Private Eye Writers of America Shamus Award; twice for the ITW Thriller Award, with one win; and once for the Mystery Readers International Macavity Award. He has also been nominated four times for the Killer Nashville Silver Falchion Award, winning it once for his novel *Paid in Spades* (Clay Stafford Books, 2019). He is a frequent contributor to Ellery Queen Mystery Magazine, along with other periodicals and anthologies. Helms' short story *"See Humble and Die"* (*The Eyes of Texas*, Down and Out Books, 2019) was selected for Houghton Mifflin Harcourt's *Best American Mystery Stories 2020*.

Brittle Karma is his twentieth novel.

Mr. Helms is a former member of the Board of Directors of Mystery Writers of America, and the former president of the Southeast Regional Chapter of MWA (SEMWA). In 2018, he was presented with the SEMWA Magnolia Award for service to the chapter.

When not writing, Mr. Helms is an avid woodworker, and enjoys travel, gourmet cooking, playing with his grandchildren, and rooting for his beloved Carolina Tar Heels and Panthers.

Richard Helms and his wife Elaine live in Charlotte, North Carolina.

Made in the USA
Middletown, DE
17 October 2021